What About Marsha?

Shye Ryder

BAER CHARLTON

Rogena Mitchell-Jones, Literary Editor
RMJ Manuscript Service LLC
www.rogenamitchell.com

10 9 8 7 6 5 4 3 2 1

Table of Contents

About

Popular lesbian romance writer, Shye Ryder, teams up with Pulitzer nominated, Baer Charlton, to bring a fresh telling of a very old refrain. With the combined introspection of Shye, and the gritty storytelling of Baer, the power of this subtle story will hit you in the gut, and make you examine your own life. This is the book people will be talking about for years to come.

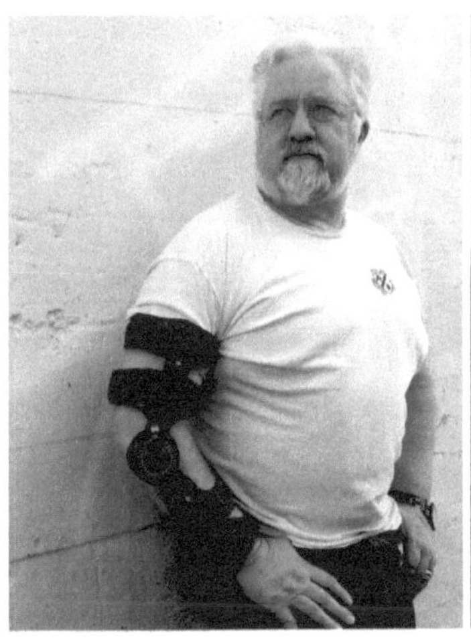 

01 Holding Daddy's Hand

SUMMER SEEMED A million miles away. Everything about it was a dream—the carefree days with the smell and bright light in the yard of freshly washed sheets hanging in the sun mixed with the pungent smell of newly mowed lawns, the blanket heat of the sunlight on exposed arms and legs—and all seemed like a movie Marsha had watched long ago.

The slow, soft, rhythmic beep of the monitor counted the pulse of her life now. Her glazed, unseeing eyes only reflected the cool rain running in rivulets down the windows, the streetlights haloing the scribbled lines. A gust of wind splattered the water into dimpled wallpaper on the glass. Her eyes blinked at the sound and movement. Her left hand absently played with the graying hair gone stringy from the third day without a shower. She sat thinking.

The oxygen at his nose sighed a continual whisper. His mouth was only a dark slice. It was enough to hear the soft wet rattle of his exhale—only a shadow of the lungs that once commanded the house and the sawyer's yard at the mill.

His voice was garbled. "I need a beer, Ellen."

Marsha held the straw to his lips. He suckled. His mind was far beyond knowing the difference between water and beer. He was a year beyond understanding the difference between his wife and his daughter. Hour by hour, it came and went.

Marsha thought about her mother. She had won. The tortured heart and body had drifted away in the night many years before.

For forty-two years, the woman had worked her body to skin stretched over tortured bone, the wife of a logger in one logging town after another. The babies were the easy part. The cooking and washing were only a challenge. Marsha remembered the holes in the pine floors from the spikes of the boots. Week after week, the Johnson floor wax filled the holes, giving a soft glow to the cheap company housing floors.

At eight, Marsha learned the arm numbing process of polishing the heat-softened wax into the holes. Crawling inch by inch on her knees, Marsha would push a wad of wax with a butter knife. She filled the holes and then went back over the entire floor to polish it to the warm glow. Her father got home and followed his habitual trek across the living room, through the dining room, and across the kitchen to the Frigidaire with the tall bottles of Coors beer. Marsha, still on the floor, could see in the late afternoon sun, the ant trail of fresh spike holes from her father's corks. He would remove those work boots just before he went to bed to sleep the sleep of the innocent.

The man, now in the hospital bed, drifted back to sleep—or whatever it was. His lips were a crack. Three slips of the pink pay-stubs would have slipped in—but not a key. His mouth had always been ready to curse or quote one of his twenty-eight favorite verses from the Bible.

In high school, Marsha had learned the truth—his verses did not come from the book. Even the chapters he quoted were not there either. It was the first time she understood the man could not read. The black leather bound book never left the small table next to his chair. The small brown plastic radio with cream knobs never played anything but his evangelistic programs. Every night at seven, and six hours on Sunday, one holy man or another shared his conversations he had with God.

The man's wife would sit in the smaller, often repaired, chair. The patches lay worn and threadbare as the original faded green fabric. Her hands moved in a steady rhythm—always filled with socks to darn or shirts to sew patches on. The socks were her husband's and sons, but the patches were good enough for the girl.

The small girl, Marsha, played with the wooden blocks the men made for their children. Every logger's child knew what a two, a four, and the long six was. The width and thickness were all the same in every logging town. A two-inch wide board had a finished thickness of three-quarters of an inch. The board was finished to one-and-a-half-inches wide. A two was as long as it was wide, a four was twice as long, and the gap-bridging six was the length of three twos. A finish was never applied. That came from the oil and grease from their children's hands. Any other finish would have required real money being foolishly spent on a child's toy.

If a girl in the company town ever got a store-bought doll, the other girls would not speak to her for many weeks. The girl could only pray her father would get a job with another company. During a move, the girl could lose the doll.

Log children knew all the things they needed to know. The value of a six, what the arched semi-circle cut in a four was for, your clothes will have patches, and if you are a girl—you and your mother's underwear would have safety pins where they hopefully didn't show. If a woman or girl's safety pin was showing, the secret code was to tell her she was looking mighty shiny that morning. If you were friends, you would go to the bathroom together so you could show her which one was showing. If you weren't friends, you only smiled—and told her nothing.

The old man moaned something, licked and then smacked his dry lips. His hand was cool and dry in hers. They said the circulation would decrease until the fingers and toes would start to die. She stared at his face. The old white scar ran from just above the left corner of his mouth, straight into the hairline above his sideburns, and past his ear. The seared line had never turned pink.

The sawpit paid more money than turning logs in the pond. As a young man, Ted had shown himself to be a good judge of a log. His eyes were quick, and he ran board footage math in his head like other men could run a woman's figure in theirs. He couldn't read, but he knew the right numbers converting a large wet log into stacks of lumber. He even knew money—but any simple arithmetic his children brought home from school was cause for him to turn on his radio show and sit staring at the distant wall as he nodded in agreement to the preaching man.

The job boss had moved him the week before into the saw shed as a stick man. The stick man would measure the butt or fat end of a log and would call out the estimated cut yield. This told the sawyer how to cut the log for the called yield and how many board feet they could count on. The sawyer was the man who would position the log to pass it through the saw. He also had the final say on any log, but they usually worked as a team. Ted had lived next door to Robert and spent as much time in Robert's backyard as Robert and his family had spent in theirs. If they were not best friends, they were close.

The fateful Friday was also the day before the spring prom. Marsha had borrowed a friend's dress. The friend had worn it the year before as a bridesmaid. Marsha didn't have a date, but it was the first dance she would be going to.

After school let out, Marsha had walked to the mail delivery. Every child knew where to take the sack with your family's name on it and exchange it for the sack with mail in it. The small children laid their hands on the counter so Rosie could stamp them with the red 'Special Delivery' or the blue 'Air Mail' ink stamps. A child in a logging camp wasn't growing up right without ink stains on the backs of their hands.

As the girls grew older, they also learned Rosie was worldlier than the other women and could help them with their hair. The two-dollars the girls paid her for the fluffy curls helped pay for all the shiny concrete in the spray bottle of hair spray.

The man had rushed into the post office and almost dove through the service window. People knew where people were, and Marsha's mother was what everyone referred to as *down mountain*.

If you were drunk in the Tri-Star bar and having an affair, you were *down mountain*. If you were doing the month's grocery shopping, you and whom you were with—were *down mountain*. If you had done run off…

Snipe Ciderrmore was a thin man nobody could imagine on the end of an ax, a whipsaw, or even one of the two-man chainsaws. He floated about the mill areas and usually was driving this or that, here and there. He was the man you would send if you needed to get a message to someone in the company town. But everyone knew Snipe's love or lust for the bottle, so sending him into the real town seventeen miles away would be tantamount to his being *down mountain* until he had slept off his drunk in the sheriff's hoosegow.

Snipe had almost shot through the delivery window. The fact that his legs were too heavy to lift saved him the embarrassment of landing in Mrs. Kallowiffski's lap.

"There were an accident in the saw shed. They done took y'all's daddy off'n the mountain—to the hospital."

The yard boss had a company truck. He offered to take Marsha down the mountain. What Marsha didn't know was the man wasn't talking about just going *down mountain* into Kernville. He was talking about going off the mountain to the city. All the way down the mountain to Bakersfield—five grueling hours of narrow winding mountain roads.

Marsha never did learn where or why her mother had been down mountain. It didn't matter. Five hours later, Marsha was completely off the mountain. The five large curls cemented to the top of her head—with the rest in beer can curlers. She wished she could forget that day, but every time she saw a can of beer, her hand would sneak to her hair.

Dark blue cloth flitted at her side. She looked up.

"How's our boy?" The nurse's voice was soft with a slight edge of an accent that might have been there as a child.

Marsha slumped slightly. "He's been in and out

most the day. More out than in, I guess."

The frost-tipped blonde nurse checked the man's pulse as she watched his respiration. Everything was on the monitor—which she ignored. Marsha almost smiled a tired curl to the lip. She watched as the woman held the man's wrist in her ungloved hand. Next, she would take a standard thermometer and stick it in the man's mouth. The routine had been the same for a hundred years, and just because a machine says it is so… Marsha liked the nurse's style. She glanced at the board. It said the nurse's name was Fred. She knew the board hadn't changed for three days.

The nurse followed her head. "Did Fred work today? He usually works the graveyard…" She groaned softly, but Marsha could hear the frustration.

The board was wiped clean. The nurse entered the right information. Marsha laughed when she wrote 'walk a six-minute mile' in the goals area. Both of them knew the man was never leaving the bed.

Marsha glanced toward her father. "In his young days on the mountains, he had a thirty-eight-inch gait and could run a mountain goat to ground. He could cover the miles to the show's slash faster than the mule team they used in those days. He carried his own ten-foot misery whip, a double-bitted ax, and his day pack. Mama said in the early days, one of the new men had a chainsaw. Daddy had dropped a double-reach before the man lost his new chainsaw in a squat. They let the other guy go."

The woman wrote the name Kit in the area for the nurse and then turned. She gently snugged the cap back on the dry marker. Her face didn't frown, but it wasn't soft. She was thinking. "What did he do…?"

Marsha smiled at the thought of someone not understanding what she had just said. All her life there was a jargon—a whole different language. Logging was as colorful and vivid as the morning cresting over the ridge in a deep fir stand. The loggers had come from many lands and languages and over generations, had built a language, which equaled where they worked and the people they worked with.

"He was a logger."

"But you said something about a show and misery."

"The company you work for has a town and a mill. The men go out to the forest and cut the trees to haul back to the mill. That is the show—all of that. But to the logger, it might just be the area he is logging, but most of the time, it is just the slash."

"Slash?"

"It's the area where the loggers take all the limbs off the logs. In those days, there was no market for limbs and pulp."

Kit leaned against the end of the bed. "I've flown over mountains where they did huge areas of clear-cut…"

"No, that's a mow… like you would mow the lawn. The mow is because almost all the trees are the same species. Out to the coast, it be Doug fir, but in the Sierras, it is more twenty-nine. That's most what daddy cut."

"Twenty-nine?"

"Species twenty-nine—is the label for white pine, spruce, and fir. The lumberyards jus' call it SPF for spruce, pine, and fir. But it's white fir instead of Doug fir. Twenty-nine is all board-stand instead of the lumber like the two-by-fours they build houses with."

Marsh realized somewhere she was leaving out information the nurse needed. Information needed for clarity about what she was talking about.

"Maybe I didn't explain—"

Kit put her hand up. "You did fine. It's all organs, and your daddy logged guts, spleen, and kidneys—but this other Doug guy was lungs and heart."

Marsha laughed softly. "Yeah, kind of like that."

Kit smiled to one side as she stood. "I'm not on for another forty minutes. The nurses said you haven't left here since about ten this morning. Why don't you come grab dinner with me? I'm only going down to the cafeteria, but you need a break and some food..."

Marsha was torn. She looked back at her father with his crack of a mouth. The eyelids didn't even flutter while Kit had taken his vitals.

Kit doubled in. "I'll buy."

Marsha blushed at the unspoken assumption. "I can afford my own way..."

Kit looked her in the eye. "That wasn't what I

meant. I meant, you really need to take a break."

Marsha stood with a last glance at her father. "Dutch." She grabbed her purse and held it in both hands like an apron.

Kit nodded with a soft smirk. She had gotten the woman to move.

02 Who is Marsha?

"WHAT ARE YOU doing here so early?"

Kit didn't have to ask the woman the same. She knew it was Saturday and the woman had been by her father's side the entire day and would be the rest of the evening. She would then be back shortly after breakfast and do it all again on Sunday.

Kit eyed the salad and small cup of coffee in front of the woman. She knew the woman could afford more and probably needed more. She evaluated the thinness of the old cardigan sweater that had patches at the elbows. She guessed it was probably bought used and had seen more than a decade of putting others first before replacement.

Kit looked at her large chicken Chinese salad and stabbed at the mass of sprouts. With her left hand, she grabbed one of the small grape tomatoes and popped it in her mouth first. She liked the way the juice felt in her mouth. The sweet tang was its own reward.

As she chewed on the salad, she pointed with her fork. It waved in the air.

"So what happened to your father?" She took a sip from the second cup of coffee of her day. Many more would follow through the night.

Marsha dabbed at the side of her mouth. Her hands

and napkin returned to her lap.

"Cancer… The smoking is prob—"

"No, when you went down the mountain."

Marsha sat back. "Oh… no… we done went *off the mountain*. There was no mountain left… we were in Bakersfield."

She thought about that time in her life. It seemed so minor now but was such a defining point at the time.

"So what happened… did a tree fall on him?"

Marsha thought about the innocent question. There were so many jobs to logging which had nothing to do with being near falling timber.

"Have you ever seen a big saw?"

Kit nodded. "One of my ex-partners did construction. There was a chop saw with a blade large enough to chop large beams." She took another bite and chewed.

"How big was the blade?"

Kit kept chewing as she held her hands in front of her chest. The size was less than two feet. Marsha snickered.

Kit wasn't sure, but the comment as she heard it sounded like the woman had said, *"City stuff."*

The tall woman stood, and extended her hand above her head. She cupped her hand as though she was holding on suspended from a bar.

"The hog blade bits would be riding in a small trough about the width of my shoe. My hand would be looped over the axle in the center, except I'm about four inches too short." She sat.

"The hog blade is almost sixteen feet across or tall. They can pass a six-foot thick log through it for a through-and-through pass. They used to have much larger blades, but trees got smaller or were cut down sooner. At one time, they used to have to split the logs into quarters to get them into the mills and onto the carrier sled. Even a thirty-foot blade could only slice twelve-foot-thick. The sawyer was worth his salt if he could square a log and harvest a ninety weight." She remembered who she was talking to.

"Ninety is the percent of weight of a wet or fresh log." She held up her clenched fist. "The bits on the teeth are this big but are only the width of my fingertip." She held up her ring finger. "The bits on the blade are moving at six-hundred miles an hour. Any faster and they would be breaking the sound barrier, and the noise would be deafening. The noise of sawing the logs is bad enough."

"Why is it called a hog blade?"

"Anything that is first to bite the log is a hog. The pincers which bite in and hold it so they can drag it out of the forest is a hog bite. If they are going to fly the log uphill, the noose on the end of the trapeze is the hog snatch. The man who readies the log is a…"

She waved the nurse to take a guess.

"The hog man?"

"No, silly. He's a logger." The two laughed. Kit liked to see Marsha let go. She could see the lines on the woman's face were more from concentration than laughing.

"They don't have a special name?"

"They do. But it would depend on the state and what kind of show. Most of the time, if it was his regular job, he would be a stringer or the flier. The man running the big engine and pulley at the top of the trapeze would be the cat man. Most of the pony engines that ran the traps were made by Caterpillar. The big engines, which were usually mounted to the back of a truck or on a railcar, were made by a company named Marmon.

"They also made the largest and most powerful trucks, so they were popular for logging. It usually took a Marmon to pull a monument out of the woods. A monument was any log large enough to be the only log on a truck. Usually, they were ten or fifteen feet across at the butt, and close to eight at the measure or small end."

"And everyone knows this language and uses it?"

Marsha started to take a bite. She paused and rested the bite of salad on the edge of the bowl. "The man who comes around to draw blood for the tests…?"

"The phlebotomist?"

She nodded as she chewed on the bite. "When dad came in, the first thing they did was put that needle in his hand and hooked him up to the drip bag thing."

Kit laid her fork down and picked up her coffee. "It's an IV drip… it was saline but could have had some glucose in it."

"And if you had to stick one of them tubes down his throat…"

"Intubation… yes, I see where you're going. We do have a lot of jargon in our forest as well. But back to the saw…"

"Have you ever put a nail in a tree and watched over the years how the bark will grow up and over the nail?"

"No… but I can imagine how it happens. The tree is growing rings each year and eventually, grows past the end of the nail and then heals the wound."

Marsha nodded. "Occasionally, someone would pound nails or a large spike into a tree. The loggers don't see the spike, but when the bit on the saw hits it…"

"Something has got to break."

Marsha softly shook her head as she remembered another accident.

"They don't break… they explode." Her lips rolled in toward her teeth. "Dad was standing where he was supposed to… it just happened to be in the wrong spot at the moment. But he was one of the lucky ones. A year later, the new sawyer was running some mortgage lifters and the bit went into his chest and pushed his heart out through his back. It flattened it against the main timber behind him. He should have known better—he was standing in the red zone."

Kit didn't need any explanation about the terms.

She understood enough for all of it. "Instant?"

Marsha held her eyes as she gently shook her head. "He was our neighbor, and the best friend daddy ever had. They worked four shows together. When it hit, he knew he was dead. He yelled to my daddy to tell his wife… but there wasn't any more breath."

The two sat quietly finishing their salads.

Death was on both minds, but the sun was trying hard to get through the slow drizzle on the atrium glass. The patterns squirming across the marble floor were like snakes. The wan sunlight made the white floor glow, but the gray of the snakes took the lightness away.

"You said you went down the mountain with him—not your mother, not we but just you. Where was your mother?"

Marsha mumbled into her salad, "She were down mountain."

Kit cocked her head sideways and frowned. "But that was where you and your father went."

"No, we went off the mountain… to Bakersfield… to the hospital. Mama was just down mountain… maybe in Kernville."

Kit squeezed her eyes closed at the two concepts which sounded the same, but the woman saw as so different. She let it go.

"Why did you go?"

"I was at the post office trying on my prom dress and getting my hair done. I was only a junior, but the school was so small, they let anyone from the junior and senior classes go."

"When was the prom?"

"That weekend…" Marsha gently placed her fork in the salad bowl. Her body was showing signs of being worn out.

Tired from more than just lack of sleep.

"So you never went to your prom…"

"No."

"But you were only a junior."

Marsha shrugged. "By the next prom, I was dating a boy from the church, and his parents didn't believe in dancing—so we didn't go."

"But you wanted to go…?"

"It didn't matter. I was Alexander's girl and what Alexander wanted… It didn't matter."

Marsha pushed the last bits of food away. "I don't want to talk about it." She looked up at Kit. The look was almost pleading.

"Are you married?"

The nurse studied the woman. "No."

"Ever…?"

"It's complicated."

"No serious relationships?"

"Sure… a couple." Kit shifted in her seat.

"But just didn't work—"

"Women…"

"They left for other women?" Marsha frowned in a question.

"One did… but the other woman and I just… well, we grew apart."

"The other woman…?" Suddenly, Marsha's eyes opened wider. "Oh…"

Kit nodded. "Yeah… it's complicated."

"Oh."

03 Judith Crystal

THE YOUNG WOMAN slouched more than sat. She leaned against Marsha with Marsha's protective arm draped over her daughter.

The subtle movement of the sheet rising and settling reflected in the young woman's eyes. Her eyes took in the mouth but didn't see the cracks on the dry lips. Only the surface was observed—nothing flowed under the topical skin.

Her voice was almost wistful in its lack of real interest or energy. "I wonder what all those numbers mean."

Marsha looked down at the top of her daughter's head. She knew her child. Her daughter didn't want a real explanation, just the cursory—simple only. "They are his blood pressure, pulse, how much air he is breathing… They mean he is dying." She stroked the head of fine dark hair. She could feel the hours of sitting in a salon—getting the hair to look like this superstar or that movie star. She didn't have to see the face to know the makeup was as perfect as one could get with only an hour to work the magic. Marsha thought about the stacks of magazines her daughter had dragged home or made her mother buy at the market. Every single issue was a collage of hair, make-up, and clothing. Every tiny detail was examined. No words, beyond titles or captions, were ever read.

Marsha leaned her head back—resting on the bunching of extra meat across her shoulders. Her body, for looks, had ended sometime in high school when she needed to get a real money job. She thought about the summer working as a housekeeper at the motel.

The Snug Bear motel was twenty-six rooms just off the main highway. Nine of the rooms were around back where a passerby could not casually see a person's car. To work there was more about turning a blind-eye to the people coming and going than how to clean or make a bed. There were days when she made the same bed two or three times on the same day.

The local businessmen found time to go do their civic duty with a philanthropic organization. Except, most days, said fulfillment of those duties were spent filling the organization's secretary or some other younger female.

At first, Marsha wanted to go tell the man's wife or at least, say something to the man. The wiser guiding hand was in the form of Tiffany, a girl two years older and many years wiser. Marsha liked working team with her. Tiffany was always showing her ways to finish faster with less work. She was also fun in a sassy way.

Marsha knew the man she almost told off that fateful day was now in a care facility and couldn't remember the day or even what he had eaten for breakfast. The Karma thing was sometimes slow, but it eventually got you.

The July heat was always thick on the body. It made the pink polyester uniform dress even hotter. The housekeepers were not supposed to run the air conditioners, but on break, Tiffany would turn on the machine under the window. She would wink at Marsha, then pull her panties down and hike up her uniform dress and sit right on the blowing cold air. Tiffany would giggle at Marsha's shocked face. Eventually, the two would take turns sitting on the appliance.

The day Tiffany spotted Marsha about to say something to Mr. Tyler and his secretary, she pulled her into the room they were cleaning and closed the door. She spun Marsha around, and with only two inches between their noses, she pointed her finger at Marsha.

In barely more than a whisper, she explained the unwritten law. "You never say a word about what you see or who you see doing it or to whom. You hear?"

Marsha blinked.

"Whoever you see… isn't here. Whoever they are with… is none of your business. You keep your trap shut and your eyes and thoughts to yourself. You hear me?"

"But what is Mr. Tyler doing here with his secretary?"

Tiffany looked deep into her face. She was chewing on her lower lip. "I'll show you—but you have to promise to tell no one. Promise?"

Marsha nodded, and Tiffany closed the small gap between them. At first, her kiss was hesitant—unsure. She felt the younger girl stiffen on the first contact. She gently grabbed at her arm. As she continued to kiss her, she felt Marsha relax and soften.

Soon, their tongues were exploring the other's mouth. Their breathing was becoming short and heated. Tiffany's hand smoothed up Marsha's uniform and cupped a stiff bra-encased breast. The bra was Sears catalog cast-iron utility restraint at best, but as the budding nipple hardened, it could be felt through the thick wall of the bra and uniform alike.

They stood panting. Their foreheads touched as they leaned into each other catching their breaths. Neither one was going to start the conversation. It was going to take more than sitting on the air conditioner to cool them down. Their eyes searched the others.

"Mama, I'm hungry."

Marsha's eyes fluttered open. She took in the hospital smells and sounds. She turned her head toward her father, but felt the weight of her daughter.

"I don't have any money, Mama. Do you have any?"

Marsha wanted to grouse about her being twenty-five and looking for a better paying job… but now was not the time. As she bent down for her purse, she mumbled in her mind. *Now is never the time—no time seems to be the right time for anything.*

She handed her daughter ten dollars. "See if there's enough for two sandwiches. If not, I guess I'll just take a yogurt cup or something."

The nurse looked over as Marsha's daughter left. Her fingers were still feeling the pulse both she and Marsha knew was already on the monitor. She watched the back side of the daughter. Her face was passively stone. The lips were drawn tight but not moving. Her brow was partially closed down, but in the lower light, it almost passed for noncommittal.

Sighing, she looked back at Marsha. The woman was unmoving. Her face was a passive challenge. This was an old fight for her.

"Which size yogurt cup did you think you will get back?"

They both knew anything but the most brutal truth would be a lie. "A sandwich with a bag of chips is seven. A yogurt cup is four, but a chocolate-chip cookie is two." She sighed. "I might see the dollar, and if she hasn't eaten it first, I might get part of the cookie."

Kit watched the monitor for a minute as she listened to the lungs. She lifted the end of the stethoscope and wound it around her head until the ends left her ears and the whole draped around her neck and down her chest. It was the mark of a nurse who performs the act dozens of times a shift—year after year.

The nurse raised her one leg, leaning and partially sitting relaxed on the end of the bed—her arms folded across her chest. Marsha knew it wasn't from disrespect of her father in the bed—it was a temporary roosting moment to make a point. It wasn't a point she hadn't told herself a million times already.

"She's my daughter. She's the baby." It said it all. It was a spineless argument, but it was the only one she had.

Kit looked at her watch. The kitchen for patient food was closed. She could only guess at when, if ever, the woman had eaten last.

She pushed off the bed and left. Minutes later, she returned with three small tubs of orange sherbet. "I'll see if I can find some kind of protein after your daughter has gone." She placed the small stack on the rolling table with a single spoon and a napkin. "These are not to be shared."

She held the hard stare and then left. Marsha looked at the sherbet. Her mind started to decide how to share it with her daughter. She sighed. *Old habits die hard.*

The blonde head peeked back in the room. "I'm serious. You eat all three now—before she comes back."

The sherbet cups were gone. Marsha had cajoled almost half of the cookie and she sat watching the young woman scroll through something on her cell phone. She had stopped asking 'what' years before.

"Don't you have to get up early for work, Judith Crystal?"

The woman looked up. Her eyes were glassy and unfocused. "What's tomorrow?"

"Monday." It always amazed Marsha that her youngest daughter was so detached. The young woman could be looking at the one instrument which showed not only the time of day but what day and date it was… and yet would ask what time it was or the day. Marsha had stopped being astounded. The young daughter had shown too many times she didn't know or even understand the concept of the fractions of the standard analog clock.

She was in high school when Marsha told her it was only a quarter till the hour—only to be answered with a blank stare. The school no longer taught students how to read an analog clock, so the fractions were meaningless. It hadn't stopped her from hinting she wanted a special wristwatch for her birthday. Marsha's Christmas bonus had almost covered the cost.

"What time do you need to be up in the morning?"

Marsha watched the thumb slide down the face of the cell phone. Most of the attention was on whatever was on the screen.

"Um… seven would be okay…"

Marsha wanted to roll her eyes. "Well, you'll need your sleep. Go ahead, and I'll be along shortly. I have my key, so don't forget to lock the front door. I'll wake you up before I leave for work in the morning."

The young woman rose as she watched the cell phone. "Mmm… okay, Mama…" She floated as much as walked out of the door. She never so much as looked back or said goodnight. The monitors pacing her grandfather winked and blinked in the lowered light. They reflected small in the single tear resting at the edge of the mother's eye.

Kit stood in the door looking down the hall. Marsha blushed and then the defensive mother took over. "Don't even start…"

Kit shrugged. "Your life—I was just wondering if there were any of them who don't have their noses welded to their phones these days." She strolled to the man in the bed and began checking his intravenous lines along with his fingertips and toes.

"My son…" Marsha sighed as she collapsed back into the chair. Her face was side-lit by the brighter light from the door. Her mind was on all of her children and how different they all were.

Kit studied the woman. Two weeks and this was new information. She had only known about the two daughters—both leeches in their own ways.

"Your son… You have a son also?"

Marsha was still distracted as she looked out at the hallway. "He doesn't have a cell phone. They're not allowed in prison."

Kit waited for the clarification. It didn't come. She straightened the bedsheets and left.

04 After Work

MARSHA GENTLY CLOSED the door on the eighteen-year-old red Toyota Corolla. She pushed it closed again. The crack was still there.

"Fuck me and a bunch of knotholes…" Her hip swung around and connected exactly where it did every one of the last few thousand times. Marsha heard the satisfying click—telling her the door was shut. Somewhere, in the hospital parking lot, she heard the chirp of another person's car locking.

She started walking with one eyelid half shut in a growl. *Mine may be old school, but it doesn't need batteries.*

Marsha stopped at the door. In the dark reflection, a woman stared back. The graying hair was tidy but no more. The clothes were presentable—for the office at the middle school. At fifty-three, the woman in the glass door mirror wasn't the woman Marsha had wanted to be so very long ago.

The high school freshman pulled on the brass handle and the large heavy wooden door swung open.

The auditorium was huge. The stage was lit bright as a couple of other students held scripts and walked quietly through their lines.

Marsha hugged her books to her chest. This was the magical place. This is where she would stop being the second-hand-me-down child and could become anything she wanted to be. This was the drama class. Not just any drama class—but theater production.

There were four older girls sitting clustered next to the drama teacher. They were talking in low voices—it was as if the class had started or at least, had been running for weeks—instead of the first day of classes. Marsha took a seat on the aisle in the twenty-ninth row. There were three students sitting farther back.

At a quarter after the hour, without even getting up from his seat or turning around, the teacher yelled out names. By the fifth name, Marsha finally understood he wasn't calling on students to quote lines—which they were—he was calling roll.

"Mason."

The boy pushing a large broom on the stage stopped. "Oh, sweet prince, how doth your cloth shine and your hair replete in the waves of the morning light…" He resumed pushing the broom.

"Mooney."

Marsha gulped and then squeaked. "Here." She couldn't think of any lines from any plays.

The four girls and teacher turned around like a silent host. Their mute stare was haunting as well as chilling. They turned around as the teacher sighed. "Yes… yes, you are."

One of the girls muttered something like, *Stage sweep*, and they all giggled or chuckled. It didn't matter. Marsha knew at that moment, those two words would define her year in drama class. She was only mostly right.

Her dust broom, like a few others, traced over the paths of the others. The theater, stage, backstage, and green room surely had to be the cleanest floors in any school. The year was one of little instruction, other than how to clean, take tickets on performance night, clean up after, and miss the 'cast' party after.

She told herself the usual stories about being too young—maybe when I can drive. My voice does not project like Cynthia's—but if I keep practicing. Then, there were the cruel ones about not being pretty enough, thin enough, smooth in movement…

The parts in plays came through the years—and were given to others.

Her senior year, Marsha landed the job of sound manager. The sum total of the job was to play a record when the main character turned to the Victrola Phonograph. The character played the phonograph three times during the play while she reclined on the swooning couch and swooned as she stared at the menagerie of glass figurines in a display case.

Marsha stood with her arm draped over the curtain master and good friend, Onna Olansofsky. The two were four-year best friends in drama. And lovers—if groping in the dark of the backstage while standing up could be considered making love.

Their eyes sparkled as they watched from the darkened stage wing. The brightly lit set was amplified to enhance Miss Caroline pant her way as she moaned or sighed deeply through her swooning.

Onna leaned over with her mouth less than an inch from Marsha's ear. Her breath was warm and scented from the two sips of Peppermint Schnapps they had imbibed in at the start of the play. "Her moaning—is she swooning from ennui or coming?"

Marsha swallowed quickly to stop from laughing. "She is panting pretty fast." She turned into the face of the other. She smiled at the eyes. "Maybe she's in labor?" She snuck a quick kiss.

Onna snickered softly, "With Mr. Branson's love child."

Marsha's mouth fell open as her eyes rolled wide. Onna took advantage and surged their mouths together and dove her tongue into the open mouth.

Marsha turned so their breasts rubbed as they kissed—

"What are you doing?" The lead actor boomed his line.

Marsha and Onna sprung apart with guilt. Quickly, she recovered and lowered the sound of the record player and faded it out.

As she dimmed the lights in the sound cabinet, a

movement in the darkest corner of the backstage caught her eye. She took one step to a dark hole which placed all the light from the stage behind her.

In the farthest dark corner were two bodies. One stood behind the other. The reflected light from the stage gave a ghostly hue to the sweating face of the balding drama teacher as he pumped at the blonde freshman with her skirt thrown up onto her back. The pale white legs were only slightly darker than the panties at her ankles.

Drama had never been that stimulating for Marsha. Marsha's fun in the dark was only fooling around with Onna.

The blonde freshman, she saw about four times a year—when she cut Marsha's hair. Neither one of them had moved very far from home. Neither woman spoke of the night in the dark. But, on the stand behind the styling chair, the two pictures in the little silver frames never changed—one of a fifteen-year-old blonde holding a baby—without the drama teacher. The other photo was of the daughter, in a cap and gown, as she graduated from college. Marsha also knew there would never be another photo of the girl. A drunk driver, on graduation night, had finished any progression.

Marsha's sight was watery. Her hand still held the large glass rod handle on the hospital door. She hadn't thought about the four years of drama in years—or of Onna and what they had done.

Marsha was looking into the eyes of a piggish

looking face. The man waited, but she could see he didn't have much patience or would suffer any foolish behavior on her part.

Marsha pulled the door open and let the man out. The man gave her a hard look. Marsha hurriedly turned away as she felt a tingling flush crawling up her neck. In her heart, she knew the man couldn't read her mind… or her memories…

Dinnertime in a hospital is the noisiest time. Marsha could hear many conversations—children of the elderly asking silly questions as if thin white hair meant the person had lost their mind or had become a child. She thought about some of the questions she had asked her own father—hoping they had not sounded silly or patronizing.

The room almost never changed. She glanced at the muted television on the wall. National news with that slender dark-haired fella—she had stopped paying attention when Peter Jennings died. There was no food on the bed table. The feeding tube erased yet another part of being a human being. The monitor to his left beeped softly, and the screen drew a jagged line of his heartbeat. The oxygen whispered its soft hiss at his nose. Everything was there for life—except the man. The booming voice, the larger than life presence, the man she grew up with had filled the house with his presence. Even when lying on the couch, taking a Sunday afternoon nap, the man filled every room in the small company house to overflowing. All of her life, his presence washed over and suffocated any persona she may produce. She was the sand under his ocean.

She glanced back at the news. She thought about how the world news and dinner defined her life. As a small girl, she was confused why Walt Disney would change his last name and read the evening news, then call himself Walter Cronkite. The night they reported he had died was the first time she had seen her father cry for seemingly no reason. She didn't understand then how he could become attached to someone he only saw on the television. Her father had been inconsolable for weeks. Finally, he had draped a bedsheet over the large old console television. It stayed covered for over a year. He had placed a photo of her mother in the middle of the expanse of white.

One day, while visiting, Marsha had placed a vase of flowers near the photo. He removed it. He didn't get mad. He explained in his quiet way how the television was only for serious matters—like the only woman he ever loved. Cut flowers were silly and wasteful. She never said a single word about how her mother loved flowers but was never allowed to bring any into the house. It was his house—even when she had moved out to start her own family, she never had cut flowers in the house.

One summer, she had placed a bouquet of flowers on the picnic table in her backyard. She had cut them from a friend's garden. She just saw a flash of someone at the table and stepped to the back door. She stood and watched as her father took the flowers and Mason jar to the trash can and dropped it in.

As he returned to the door, he explained, "Some fool dropped off some silly flowers. I cleared them for you." As he ignored the look of shock on her face, he climbed the two steps and wormed past her. "I need a beer."

She and her husband may have paid the rent, but since they rented from her father, it was still his house and he would have his say. There was beer in the cooler, so the Coors was his to drink as well.

She looked at the red plastic clock over the sink. It was a quarter till noon. As she softly closed the back screen door, she knew she would be expected to make him something to eat as well.

She leaned against the door frame of the hospital room. Even in the last ninety-pounds of a wasting body, his presence filled the room. Marsha stepped back as she felt herself suffocating.

05 Brother and Fathers

THE WOOD AND metal cafeteria chair across from her pulled out. Marsha slowly opened her eyes and looked up. It took a moment to realize who was sitting down.

She smiled tiredly at the nurse. "Going off, coming on, or just taking a break?"

Kit raised one eyebrow. Her hands were gently gripped in her lap. She studied the slightly older woman. "Even with all the bloodletting around here, we do get lunch."

Marsha looked at the empty table in front of the nurse. "Hmm, I see you are on that new air diet…"

Kit's face pulled back on one side. "Walking dead, and you can still crack a smartass joke."

Marsha leaned over to her left as she combed her hair with her fingers. Her head came to rest on her palm. The sigh was more from her exhausted body than a breath. "It was just a long day at the school. We had a child take some of his mother's drugs and had to call the paramedics."

The nurse listened to how the news was delivered and read the body language. "And this happens how often…?"

Marsha sighed, blowing out her lips. "God… these days…? I think this was the third time this month. Some months, nothing happens, then school starts and the craziness gets rolling. Kids with guns, kids with drugs, kids in a group beating a smaller kid, gang-rapes at twelve… heck, smoking in the bathrooms is the least of our worries these days."

She sat upright but then slouched in her chair. She yawned.

"I remember when my brother got caught smoking out behind the gym. Daddy like to strip the hide from his bottom with the razor strop."

"I didn't know you had a brother."

Marsha's lips rolled in toward her teeth as she thought about her older brother. "Max… after the boxer, Max Baer. He was a few years older than me." She had hated him as much as she looked up to him. He never treated her bad. He never picked on her. Never hit her like some other boys did. Never did much of anything except ignore the only sister he would ever have.

"He was a Marine. The only items we got back from Somalia were a new set of dog tags and a purple heart."

Kit sunk a fraction into the chair. "I'm sorry…"

Marsha took a deep breath and sat up, then leaned back into the chair. The tiredness was obvious, and it wasn't from just a long day. "Don't be… it was a long time ago." She frowned. "Are you going to eat or not?"

"I'd better go get it. It should be done now."

Marsha yawned as she watched the blue scrubs walk away. Many wore the lighter blue, but she liked how the darker blue color with the spiky dark blonde hair and frosted tips. Most nurses wore scrubs baggy—like a pair of pajamas, but Kit's were more form-fitting or tailored like real clothes.

She blushed and hurriedly looked around to see if anyone had noticed her watching the younger woman. Nobody was paying any attention.

She picked up her fork and stabbed at the small salad. The cherry tomato jumped out of the bowl. Her left hand stopped it at the edge of the table. She held it a moment, considering the five-second rule—and then popped it in her mouth. Old habits of economics won over cleanliness. She figured the tabletop in a hospital cafeteria should be as clean as the counter of her kitchen. She chewed methodically as she thought about her brother.

A lettuce wrapped sandwich and a cookie on a plate pushed the small salad bowl aside. "Here. It's my own creation—grilled skinless chicken fingers with julienned veggies in a wilted lettuce wrap. It was my secret weapon in losing over half my body weight. But, beyond that—it tastes good, too."

Marsha looked at the wraps. "You lost how much?"

Kit sat down with a smirk. "Let's just say… well over a hundred pounds."

Marsha sat back stunned. "Holy Toledo…"

Kit took a bite of her wrap and nodded. Talking with the bite shoved in cheek. "Yeah, as well as half of Cincinnati, the lower half of Chicago, and most of Denver… there was a lot of me to go around."

"How… what…?"

"How did I lose it, or how did I put it on? Losing wasn't easy, but it was better for me than putting it all on."

The blonde took another bite and chewed. "Long relationship number two wasn't healthy for me. There are many ways to abuse someone which have nothing to do with hitting them. I know it now—but didn't then. My defense was to pack on weight. It's called shielding or armoring. Many dykes do it, but not usually because of the relationship they are in. Usually, both partners do it together." She took another bite.

"Why?" Marsha chewed and held up the wrap and nodded.

"Good, huh?" Kit took a sip of water. "In a relationship, you tend to date people you look like. Blondes dated blondes, brunettes with brunettes, tall with tall, and well… you get the picture. But let's say you and I start dating, and I'm a size four, and you're a size eight or ten. We aren't a match. So the easiest way is to both become a size twelve or fourteen. The problem is, once you start down the slippery slope, and you're staying home instead of going to the gym or other activities…"

Marsha rolled her eyes. "Starchy comfort food, and we'll get fat together."

"Worse. If you're fat, who are you to tell your partner they're fat? And besides, you worked hard to find someone, so why would you risk a fight and break up?"

"So you two got fat together…"

Kit shook her head and swallowed as she wiped a bit of food off the side of her mouth. "Not after the first year. Connie was having an affair, and started cutting back on the food. She didn't want me to take part in her sports, so she made my dinner portions larger. Soon, she found out by nagging me about being a whale, I would eat even more to feel better. The rocky road appeared in the freezer, and I never questioned it. Doughnuts left on the counter, one was missing, but I never thought to look in the garbage. Finally, she stuck the knife in and twisted…"

"She moved out."

"That would have been more humane. Nope—she moved me into an apartment and moved her new girlfriend in with her."

Marsha sat with her mouth open. She had no idea the world of homosexuals was so much like the rest of the world. Logically, she knew everybody was just people—but she somehow thought those kinds of relationships would be… more civil or better somehow.

Kit could read the woman's face. She smiled sadly. "What, you didn't think bastards could come in different sexes?"

"So what did you do?"

"What could I do? Fight for a relationship that had been seven years of poison? Fight to get back the woman I thought I loved, but who didn't love me? I didn't have a choice—I went home."

"Home?"

"To my folk's house—moved right back into the bedroom and bed I had left twelve years before. Curled up under the blanket with my belly hanging out in front and my fat ass airing out the back and had a week long pity party."

She wiped her hands on the napkin and folded it neatly and placed it on her plate. "The folks went on with their lives like I wasn't there. In the middle of the night, I would sneak downstairs and scarf through a half box of Cheerios with gobs of sugar. When the cereal ran out, I switched to cooking rice. The next night, the large bag of rice was gone. I looked in the refrigerator, and there was a bowl of fruit with a note on it from my dad. It said if I wanted to kill myself, I needed to go do it somewhere else. But if I wanted some fruit, here it was. It was signed dad—with a heart in red for the *a*.

"I just collapsed right there and bawled until he

came in the kitchen. He just plopped down on the cool linoleum and held me. He whispered in my ear that electricity was expensive, and he had come in to close the fridge. Hugs were free. That is how my dad is. He sat there until the sun came up, just rocking me and calling me his Kit Kat.”

“Sounds like a loving guy.”

“He was… but about some things—like wasting electricity, he was pragmatic.

Uncomfortable with the intimate nature, Marsha changed the conversation. “You mean Kit isn’t a nickname?”

Kit laughed. “As a little girl, Dad thought Christina was too grown-up. So he called me Kit Kat like the chocolate bar. He would sing the jingle about breaking off a piece and would pretend to eat my fingers or toes. It was always a way to get me to laugh. I started calling him Goofy or Goof Ball. It all stuck. I was Kit Kat, and he was Goof Ball.”

She pushed the plate to one side and rocked in on her elbows. “After I had lost over a hundred pounds, he looked at me one morning and said because I was only half the woman I used to be—he could only call me Kit. That was over ten years ago, and he hasn’t called me anything else since.”

“I’d love to meet him. He sounds very nice.”

“He’s over on the coast at Oxnard Home. He is in the final stages of Alzheimer’s. Until last year, my name tag would help him. Now, even my telling him doesn't help—so I'm just another nice nurse who will sit with him and fluff his pillow or take him out into the sunshine."

Marsha started to say something and then stopped. "I was going to say how sad. But… then I thought about how similar we are…"

A wan smile slid across Kit's face. She checked her watch and stood. "I think we have a lot more in common than you know."

Marsha sat and chewed meditatively, watching the nurse walk across the cafeteria. The assured walk and weaving around the tables filled with other diners reminded her of her father and brothers. The three men had been so much alike. The world was theirs but in simple terms. There was no treading careful ground. No avoiding land mines of *do and do not*. Their footprints were secured by who they were, and it was never in dispute.

Along the outer edge of the tables, a woman gently pushed a man in a wheelchair. She was talking low as if they were quietly sitting in a garden or somewhere quiet. The man was staring slack-jawed at the floor as if he were counting the tiles as they softly slid by under the wheelchair.

The scene shimmered, and Marsha could smell the hospital garden in Bakersfield the year she was sixteen. The summer heat on the plants was pungent. The plants barely flourished against the heat before they died and rotted. Everything was sweaty from the misting sprinklers hopelessly fighting against the heat and dryness of the Central Valley. The bandage on his head was a large ball of white—floating above the hard shoulders of her father.

Marsha pushed him toward the small raised pond. The wall was made from red bricks baked to tan in the sun. In the middle of the pond were lily pads. One had a flower. They sat, not talking. Marsha ran her hand in the water. A fish silently swam by deep in the water. The shadows played along the silver and orange of the fish. It was there, but as it swam, it changed and became a retelling of the old fish as it became a new fish.

She looked at her father. His eyes were watery. They were slewed to the left, not looking at anything in particular—just slewed to the one side. She thought about telling him to look at the one flower. She thought about explaining about the fish. She knew none of it mattered… anything she was drawn to was not what he paid attention to in his world.

She sat on the wall around the pond. Her hands quiet as her mouth rested unmoving in the lap of her dress. It was the sixth day she had worn the dress without washing it. She sighed deeply. The stench of the rotting garden burned in her nose. She sat… beside her father with a white basketball of gauze for a head. She could feel the unclean fabric on her skin.

She turned her head and looked at the sky to the west. There was nothing there.

06 You Had Another Brother?

THE MONITOR WAS passively blinking. The soft, ever-present, beep filled the room. Marsha leaned against the doorjamb—watching the young nurse attend to her father. Marsha could tell by the nurse's movements how much she did not care about the man in the bed. This young woman had taken the schooling to get a job. This was not a calling, a holy undertaking of caring for the less able of the world. She would do what was necessary to get the paycheck on Friday.

The nurse wore baggy pajama type scrubs. The dogs playing on the top may have been cute for a children's ward but, in Marsha's mind, unprofessional where people were dying. The cutesy top was either cheaper or the young woman loved dogs and brought her love to work with her. Marsha wondered if there were any scrub tops with injured and sick or dying humans printed on them.

She could hear the soft dry rasping of the nurse's pantyhose in the scrubs. She wondered about a woman who wore pantyhose under her pajamas. Even if they were extra-heavy-duty control-top, they would do nothing to hide the size of the young woman. Marsha sneered in her mind—*she was not fooling anyone but herself.* Marsha knew the type. They laughed too fast and too loud. They were the fun ones who went home and cried long and hard as they emptied the ice cream carton in the dark of the night.

The nurse bent slightly to tuck in the lower corner of the sheet hanging almost to the floor. If she had paid any attention, she would have noticed the other corner was only covering half of the man's other foot. She wadded up the extra sheet and shoved it under the mattress. The nurse was panting from the slightest effort. Marsha was sure she was also sweating from arranging the bedsheet.

Marsha watched the old man's limp face. His eyes were closed, but she could see the bumps of his eyes rolling back and forth—watching the sounds of the nurse. Marsha knew he would have called it fussing over him. From the stillness of his hands, she also knew he was holding himself in tight control. It was the quiet control he would draw himself into just before he would let fly with his belt when they were kids. The man said he never swung the belt in anger—to do so was to lose in the war of being a parent. Anger, in his mind, led to over whipping children and was wrong.

Marsha wondered briefly what he would have to say about beating one's wife.

He didn't care if he had fresh sheets. The same as

he hadn't cared about his daughter wearing the same dirty dress for three weeks, nor where she was staying. The only cleanliness the man ever cared about was his dinner plate and his relationship with his god. Everything else could be as dirty as the cracks in his hands or the moonshine he and Herb McCracken made from the crushed field corn until Herb went blind from a bad batch.

The nurse held his wrist and watched the monitor. Marsha knew that checking the wrist told her more about how the man was doing then the monitor could. Sometimes old school was better.

As the nurse passed by her, she rolled her eyes and shook her head with a small smile. "He ain't fooling nobody. He ain't sleepin'. He as awake as we is—he jus' being cantankerous as an old goat."

Marsha winked with a tired smile. "He is an old goat. But he's my old goat."

Marsha watched the man lying there. The chest slowly rose and fell in an even, relaxed rhythm. His left hand had resumed plucking at the bedsheet. She thought about how chilly it was the last evening. She decided to go out to the car and fetch her sweater. She rolled off the doorjamb and paused. The fire escape at the other end was closer to the parking lot. She turned left and walked past the nurse's station.

She waved shyly at Kit, who was just coming on. Marsha glanced at her watch. The Timex had been her mother's and still kept good time. It was quarter till eight.

Several minutes later, she pulled herself up the fire stairs. She hated stairs—they would brutally tell you you're not twenty-years-old anymore. Stairs are faster to the truth than any friend, enemy, or family. Her right knee, where as a young girl she had been kicked by a tree, was acting up.

She had just turned twelve, and her father had taken the family out into the forest. The word he had used was picnic—but the basket in the back of the battered old Ford pickup sat alongside three chainsaws, gas cans, gloves, and hard hats. They had come to drop some trees for fall firewood. Marsha never heard the term businessman's holiday, but she did know her father.

After spending six days working in the forest or around logging, for him to bring his tools on what was supposed to be a family outing of fun… something was up, and it wasn't just the sky.

Marsha could smell the grease from the fried chicken. Her mother melted the Crisco and stirred in fresh chopped wild rosemary and fennel. She had also smelled her mother baking biscuits shortly before serving the family a breakfast of Cream-O-Wheat. They would be in the basket with honey stolen from the black tree behind the Rucker's house. Her mother's shortbread biscuits had won ribbons at the county fair and jealousy at the church potlucks.

The lunch in the forest was as good as it always

was. Marsha's mother was a good cook. The chicken was crispy on the outside, yet sweet and juicy on the inside. The biscuits with honey were light and fluffy. The dirty rag, soaked in the cold stream water, lying across her swelling knee was still painful. She had limped in pain for weeks.

Her father, as a logger, insisted all of his children know how to fall a tree. Her brother had chosen his own tree which was as thin as his arm. It took almost as long to pull the trigger on the chainsaw as it did to cut through the trunk. Her father had chosen her tree for her—it was as thick as his thigh. The whippy green cedar sapling was full of wind catching greenery.

The wind gusted sideways at the worst moment. The steering cut cracked to the right instead of falling straight out. As the tree toppled, the cut trunk dropped sideways—hinging off the uncut side. The cut butt swung off the high attachment of the hinge, striking her in the knee. She was thrown off her feet, and the end of the still roaring chainsaw churned its way into the forest floor. The chain bound and shattered. The chunks tore into the still roaring engine.

In the sudden forced silence… Marsha could only hear her father swearing. The sound of her father swearing in the calm of the forest faded into the quiet of the hospital hallway.

Marsha pulled on her sweater as she walked past the nurse's station. Kit waved her over.

"Someone is in there."

Marsha frowned, "Who?"

Kit shrugged and made a face. "I don't know. Lawyer type—briefcase and all…"

Marsha groaned. *Insurance assholes*. She gripped the top of Kit's hand. "Thanks for the heads up. I owe you one."

Kit snorted with a smirk. "I'll take a double shot espresso with Bailey's…"

Marsha understood the sentiment. She turned and kept moving.

The briefcase was a dark red. It rested on the roll-around bed table as if it were holding court. The red glowed with a soft shine—as if polished at a shoe shine stand. The three gold initials would never need polishing—pure gold never tarnishes. Marsha even knew when the initials were hot stamped into the leather. The briefcase had cost Marsha more than when she bought her six-year-old Toyota two-door. The list of who passed the bar exam had been posted less than an hour before, but Marsha had been making layaway payments on the briefcase for over a year.

Marsha looked at the closed door to the toilet. She knew her oldest daughter never passed up a chance to spread her poop around to new places in the city. She was sure the young woman on some level saw it in the same light as a dog marking its territory. As a child, she had pooped in changing rooms. She adorned bedrooms of relatives she didn't like. Clothing she didn't like. She would then leave it hidden or use it to smear in an out-of-the-way place. Once, she even took off her panties to poop on the pew at the church she hated attending. The family had never gone to church again, not even for Midnight Mass on Christmas.

Marsha took a deep breath and gently closed her eyes. She walked to the chair closest to the inconvenient reason for everyone having to visit. Marsha patted her father's hand and muttered for him to just keep pretending to sleep. She set her purse on the floor and then took off her cocoa-cream cardigan with the leather patches her mother had sewn many years before. She folded the sweater and placed it over her purse. She then folded back her sleeves to appear as if the temperature in the hospital was normal or even a bit warm. She smirked as she knew her daughter dressed in three layers of clothing as she was always cold. It was the nature of a reptile.

She rolled her eyes and plopped into the chair to wait.

Her closed eyelids twitched at the sound of the door latch.

She could hear the sound of hands being wiped in a large wad of paper towels.

"I'm not sure the cleaning staff cleaned in here today. I've seen cleaner facilities in third world countries. I didn't trust the seat even with a double paper liner, and the paper towels may have been a bit too much for this old of an institution's plumbing. Maybe they should send the facilities person up here and have them do whatever it is they do to make it work again."

Marsha sighed but didn't move. "Hello, Tiffany Anne. The cleaning crew was here at four this afternoon. Yes, once again you have successfully clogged the toilet in a place you will never be in again and will be leaving in less than five minutes. The hospital is younger than you are, but I will call the staff after you have left so you don't suffer the unjustified position of being embarrassed."

"Oh… hello, Mother." She looked around to where she could dispose of the last five paper towels she needed to safely open the toilet door. She gave up and placed them in the small sink the nurses used to wash their hands every time they entered the room or after handling a patient.

She approached and clasped her hands on the briefcase above the handle. "I've got to get back to work… but I stopped in to say hello to grandpa… but he's sleeping." Her hand moved down to the handle.

Marsha stared at her daughter. The wool suit probably cost more than Marsha thought she ever had loose in the bank. She didn't have to look to know the purse and shoes matched the deep muted red of the briefcase. The rail-thin figure showed no signs of womanhood—much like the personality, which was also incapable of showing signs of emotion or empathy.

Marsha had worked in the evenings after the kids had gone to bed, to sew her oldest a prom dress. The dress matched a dress on the cover of a magazine. When she presented her daughter with the hand sewn dress, her daughter's only comment was that she hoped it would fit and not make her look ridiculous. The woman on the magazine was Princess Diana.

It was the last dress Marsha ever sewed.

Marsha could sense the silent tapping of a mental foot.

She slow-blinked her eyes as she looked away to her father. The soft light made the white sheets appear yellowish-gray. "Maybe next time…"

She could hear the briefcase being lifted, not dragged. Her daughter grunted a hum and the heels clicked softly but with a strident gait.

Marsha sat leaning onto her left arm as her hand rubbed at her forehead.

She could hear a cart of some kind pass down the hall. The soft squeak of the hospital shoes followed.

Marsha breathed deep and sighed as she slouched into the chair and rested her head back.

"Is the ice queen gone?"

Marsha chuckled softly. "Yes, Dad… It's safe to come out now."

The old man took a slightly deeper breath from the cannula at his nose. His eyes were still shut. "Do you remember the nurse they had there at your school?"

Marsha snorted softly. "Do you mean the nurse at the Oakdale high school…? The one who wore the tight white dresses and oversized paper hat…?"

His nod was barely more than a twitch.

Marsha snorted. "She wore her dress tight enough to stop a real person from breathing. We used to laugh how you could count all of her ribs from the back. Danny Taylor once joked how the doubled up control hose were so tight if she farted—it would blow her shoes straight off. Connie Tate and I once saw her walking up the rear fire steps. We could see up her dress a ways. We about died laughing because if the double stockings weren't enough—she had one of them JC Penney's longline extra-hold girdles on too."

The man wasn't laughing. "You weren't a parent then. Your mother used to make me deal with her when you kids were hurt or sick. She had a way… She could just freeze your heart and make your water turn black."

Marsha thought about her daughter and then remembered her younger brother. "She must have been extra special when Junior broke his arm in football."

Her father rolled his head, and one eye opened. "I never had to deal with her about that. If I had…" He rolled back and closed his eyes. "I think I would have left your brother where he sat."

"But you had to pick him up…"

"I worked with the coach's daddy. The coach called the mill. We was shootin' the cinder tower. Cleveland was top man in the cone and runnin' the blaster. It was noisier than standing next to the thirty-foot blade of a sawyer's table, and you know how I hate loud noise. Coach told the office person to get his daddy—there had been an accident. It took Cleve ten minutes to turn the blaster off and climb down from the scaffolding. It were another hour for us to beat it back to town." He paused to suck on the oxygen at his nose. Marsha could hear the wet congestion softly gurgling in his chest. She knew it was the true beginning of the end.

"Coach had set your brother at the end of the bench until we came and got him. He didn't fetch Junior an ice bag or nothin'. If he fetched any ice, he would have to tell the nurse. Even he were afraid o' that there nurse."

"If I remember right, the bone was sticking out of his skin…"

The man nodded. "It were. Coach got in his face while he were still lying hurt on the field. Told the boy if'n he cried, coach would have to give him to the nurse, and he would be off the team. Junior never dropped so much as a single tear."

Marsha noticed the pulse was up at least twenty points. His blood pressure could use lowering, but nobody was worried about his long-term care.

Marsha hadn't heard Kit come in. The nurse removed the damp paper towels from the sink and walked them over to the trash can against the wall. At the sound of the metal lid, Marsha turned around and smiled.

Kit scrubbed her hands as she watched the man in the bed through the mirror. There wasn't much getting past her attention. She rinsed and performed a shortened repeat washing. Drying her hands on a single paper towel, she walked over to look down at the man in the bed. "I didn't know you had a second son, Mr. Mooney." She looked to Marsha for the answer, "Older or younger?"

Marsha gave a soft smile. "This one was the baby. His name was Paul, but we always called him Junior because he was junior to everyone else in the family. He's a Chief Petty Officer now in Norfolk, Virginia."

Kit held the old man's wrist as she watched the monitor. "What kind of ship?"

Marsha mussed, "I think they used to call them frigates, but he calls it a light destroyer. All I know is they're using missiles now instead of cannons on his ship. Junior is in charge of the launch control center. He likes those computers and stuff. I have enough problems with just using a phone these days."

The nurse watched the old man's breathing as she talked. "I hear you. I was still fine with my old flip phone... until mine got thrown at my head two years ago."

"Ouch..." Marsha winced.

Kit walked around the end of the bed. She wore a smirk. "I got rid of the flip phone, Sprint, and my girlfriend all in the same day. I've been a single girl in a relationship with AT&T ever since." She winked as she raised the head of the bed a few inches. She turned to the old man. "That should make it easier to breathe,

Mr. Mooney." She patted his leg. She watched his breathing, and it did appear to be less of a struggle. The wet flutter became more of a damp flutter and quieter.

As she turned and walked past Marsha, her face was serious. She slowly shook her head as her lips rolled in. The end was starting.

07 What Else

PAPERWORK HAMMERED HER desk and her day. The district office had requested a review of all the students who came from struggling families. The scope covered single parents, those on welfare, broken or breaking homes, as well as children living with a grandparent.

The one category they didn't have to say was children of an imprisoned parent or parents. Marsha was already familiar with where those fell in the system. She was all too familiar with how many children walking the halls, looking forward to or dreaded the next visiting day at whichever prison. Whether it was the women's prison in Vacaville or the men in Soledad and San Quentin over in the Bay Area, or just the county lockup for the lesser offenders, it was still a draining process on the children. She saw the hollow stares every day at her counter.

How well she remembered dropping the two girls off at her mother's the night before. Even the summer months didn't make the before dawn drive to San

Quentin prison any warmer. Recalling the pat-downs by the matrons still made her skin crawl. She prayed to be hit hard enough in the head to get amnesia and forget the three times she was strip-searched. She was sure the two matrons who barely hid their giggling at the cowering woman were the same ones who laughed at her in drama. There was no dignity left from a visit to see her son.

The principal had left at six. The paperwork was still thick stacks on her desk. His stopping for a second on his way home to dinner would have been considerate if he hadn't quipped to work quickly and not to stay too late. She knew his only concern was the overtime. There had been no offer to help—not by him, not by any of the other office staff, and not the district office with an extension or reasonable time frame.

THE LETTUCE IN front of her looked like the form DSE-471-3—the washed out green with sprinkles of blue or red.

A fuzzy thought floated heavily through the back of her mind. The district office could afford forms in triplicate or even the annual review forms in quintuple—but the schools had to use the… She cocked her head. Did they still use mimeograph…? The chemical smell hung pungent but sweet in her memory.

The chair across from her pulled out. The dark blue

form sat. "You don't have to hurry. He's pretty out of it tonight. They sucked the mucus from his upper lungs and esophagus this afternoon, and they had to mildly sedate him. He's groggy and sort of drifts in and out."

Marsha watched the blonde. She knew recognition would kick in soon. The words were slow to take form. She blinked as it all fuzzily made sense. "Thanks, Kit."

The nurse part in Kit joined her woman part, who had come to know Marsha enough to care. She watched the eyes slowly track. She evaluated the picked at salad. Her lips rolled in as she realized the woman's sweater was still on. There was a small skid trace of salad dressing on the front of the sweater. She figured the physical piece of salad was in the lap. The woman was either half dead or three-quarters asleep.

"Should I just call you a cab… or would an ambulance be a better choice?" She leaned in and took the left hand which was resting on the table. "Sweetie, your father won't know if you didn't see him tonight. But you need some sleep."

Marsha gently shook her head as she rallied. "It was just a very long day…"

Kit raised an eyebrow. "Would coffee even help?"

The head almost approached a semi-quick snap up. "Oh… coffee…"

Kit snickered as she rose. She patted Marsha on the shoulder as she walked by. "I've got this. You keep eating."

Marsha sipped the coffee with the one ice cube in

it. It felt good and washed down the bite of salad. She took another quick sip and set down the cup. "Thanks, it does help."

"Well, at least I don't have to check your pulse." Kit chewed on her wrap as she watched the woman eat her salad. "So ten at night… what happened at school?"

Marsha mumbled around her food and then swallowed. "The district asked for reports on several kids. It was all stuff they should have been paying attention to all along. I think there is a lawsuit coming or an investigation. They usually don't care about kids until they are either being or they feel threatened."

"Which kids?"

Marsha started to chase the last of the small salad around the bowl. Two pushes and she dropped the fork in the plastic bowl and pushed it all away from her. "Too much work." She looked up, thinking about what Kit had asked. She pinched her nose between her thumb and knuckle. Rubbing the nose together, she gave it a soft itching. "It's complicated, but basically, they needed reports on the kids who live in households with only one parent. They are trying to map the ones who are at risk of dropping out once they get to high school."

"Does it work?"

"Tracking them…?" She shrugged softly. "It might. I think if they reduced the class size and paid more attention to the kids, they would have better results. But first, you have to get the parents to pay attention and spend more time with their kids."

Kit watched her. "Is that what happened with your kids?"

Marsha's eyes rolled wide. "Oh, who knows? I think the last civil conversation I ever had with my son was when he and I baked a cake together for Cub Scouts. The next week, he was running around with a bad crowd, and I never got anything but a screaming match. You've met the girls."

"I forgot you had a boy... how did he turn out?"

"We'll find out in thirteen more years when he gets out of San Quinton. That's assuming Tim doesn't beat up a guard... again."

"Beat up a guard?"

"He went away for five-to-seven. He was almost staying out of trouble until they came in to toss his cell. He exploded out of his sleep and beat the guard's head against the wall. He would have probably killed the man, but the other guards took him down. He was in the prison hospital for three months while his hearing went to the board, and his sentence was extended to twenty years on top of his five. He has an explosive temper."

"If you don't mind me asking... what did he do to get sent to prison?"

Marsha rolled her eyes. "Beat up a security guard where he worked. The man reached for Tim's lunch pail to search it and he exploded. Everyone's pail or bag gets searched. He knew it, and it happened every day. But one day, it was just the wrong day."

"It sounds like he has a problem with guards…"

Marsha flattened her lips like a duck as she twitched her head no. "Uniforms—he beat up a few of the band members in school. We had to pull him off one of the mailmen once. We thought he might have learned his lesson when the post office replaced the guy with an ex-Marine. Tim jumped him, and actually got a couple of feet away before the guy's fist connected with Tim's nose. It dropped him cold to the sidewalk. The mailman stepped over him like he was a child's tricycle or something and handed me the mail. He never said a word about it."

Kit's eyes were large, and her face was ready to laugh. "What did you do?"

Marsha started chuckling. "We stuck some plastic straws up his nose before he came to and packed it with toilet paper. When he could get up and walk, I took him to the doctor. When we got there, he almost couldn't see. The doctor cut down the straws and changed the packing. Said I had done a good job and sent us home. I kept icing it, and after a couple of days, he could see a little out of the left eye."

Their laughter echoed in the empty cafeteria.

Marsha sipped the last of her coffee. She was feeling more alive. "What about you?"

"What about me?"

"Growing up… siblings…? I keep rattling off, and then when I'm driving home, I realize I don't know nothing about you."

"Sister. She was older."

Marsha collapsed and hung like a rag doll with wide eyes. "That's it. I pour my heart out, and all I get back is an older sister?"

Kit shrugged and chuckled. "Pretty much… She was seven years older than me and grew up in the same mentality you did. She married her high school sweetheart, had two kids, and got a divorce. Her second husband put her in the hospital four times before she shot him."

Marsha started. "She shot him?"

"No, just checking whether I had put you to sleep yet." They both chuckled as they gave each other the eye. "She didn't shoot him, but she should have. He did put her in the hospital, though. The last time she was brought in, he was stupid enough to tell the nurse she had fallen down the stairs. The nurse knew them. She lived down the block and knew the one step front stoop in front of the single story house wouldn't have done the damage. She placed a call to the x-ray department but had dialed the hospital security. They called the cops. He left the hospital in handcuffs, but my sister refused to press charges. That was when I stopped talking to her."

"Was anything done about the… the husband?"

Kit lowered one eye. "I never liked her first husband because he always made remarks about gay people should be wiped off the face of the earth… but he did go visit, the jerk. I guess he got arrested, but the district attorney didn't see the fight beyond two drunks. Fred, husband number one, got a broken nose and a few cuts from a broken bottle. Husband number two still walks funny from having his knees broken and the one hip doesn't work right anymore. Baseball bats will do that to you sometimes."

"Ouch." Marsha shifted in her seat. "I heard about a logger who took his chainsaw to his wife's lover once… but I think it was called assault with a deadly weapon. Where did you grow up?"

"San Fernando Valley. Van Nuys to be exact. We didn't have chainsaws." Kit glanced at her watch and shook her head. "I've got ten minutes more."

"What about your sister?"

"The last I heard, she was working on the next ex-mister number four. I heard they were somewhere down in one of the beach towns. I really don't pay attention anymore."

"But she's your sister…?"

Kit finger combed her hair back and turned her head. The scar running from behind her ear down along her jaw was narrow and not obvious. "There was a time when I was stupid enough to go to lesbian bars. One night, a fight broke out. I wasn't even part of it, but the full bottle of some whiskey made me one of the casualties. It shattered my jaw in four places. The cops who broke up the fight found me slumped over the end of the bar and figured I was just drunk. I had the matron call my sister from the holding cell to ask her to come take me to the hospital." She let the hair fall back in place. "She told the matron I had chosen my lifestyle, and I could call a dyke to clean me up."

"Ouch…"

Kit nodded. "I've never spoken to my sister since."

"But you did get to a hospital…?"

"The matron called her girlfriend. I still don't know if there was a fine they paid or not. If I saw either one on the street, I still don't think I would recognize them. I'm not even sure if they were lesbians or not… it didn't matter." She rolled her hand over on the table. "One of those random acts of kindness of strangers. I try to pay it forward here and there, but down deep… you know you will always be indebted to them."

"So you stopped drinking?"

"I like a glass of wine now and then. I like to barbecue and I'm a little strange, but I like a sweet Riesling to balance my homemade honey and Worcestershire barbecue sauce."

"That's it… just honey and worsty?"

"If I'm feeling dangerous, I throw a few packets of ketchup in there too. I brought home a few packets of Caesar dressing once… once." She screwed her face up and pushed her tongue out. "It is not the same as the blue cheese thing they do out at Tagus Ranch House. Their Blue Cheese steak is to die for." She stood looking at her watch. "You really should just go home."

Marsha stood and collected her plate and purse.

"I'll just come up for a minute. If he's truly out, I'll go home… I promise."

"I'm going to hold you to your word."

As they approached her father's room, Kit reached out and squeezed Marsha's shoulder. "I'll check in and be right back."

Marsha nodded and walked into the darkened room. The soft nightlight allowed her to see her father. She could tell by his face he was not happy, but he was asleep. It always amazed her how a person could be asleep and still have an upset look on their face. But then, she thought about her oldest daughter. Even as a child, a sour look seemed to always be on her face— sleeping or awake. Marsha wondered what face she wore as she slept. She thought about Kit at dinner and how quick she was to smile or laugh. She wondered if Kit slept with a smile.

"Looks like no change. He'll sleep through until breakfast." Kit's arm slid over Marsha's shoulder and gently turned the woman toward the door.

Marsha reached around and side-hugged her. "Thank you, Kit, for being a great nurse, and also for being a friendly ear. I don't know what to do some days…"

Kit leaned her head on the other. "This is not easy for anyone. I've been here many times, and it's never easy. The best I can be for the family is at least friendly. Most have family who gathers in and provides strength… but you don't, so you get me. Now go home.

It's Friday night, and I've left word with the front desk to shoot you on sight if you're here before two in the afternoon."

Marsha hugged her again. "Thanks. I'll see you tomorrow."

Kit stood leaning against the doorjamb as she watched the woman walk the hall. At the elevators, she paused and turned. She gave a small wave before stepping into the opening and was gone.

Kit paused—listening to the man's breathing. The wet rattle was less, but still there. She had read the chart. His last intake of food was three days before. Soon, they would switch from glucose to just hydration on the intravenous, and even then, reduced. The day nurse had installed the catheter the day before. Everything was down to palliative care and waiting.

08 Losing a Grip

INTERSTATE 5 IS mind numbing. The two lanes of sun faded asphalt are what colorists call photo-gray. The color, in most circumstances, will fade away when any other color is introduced. Unfortunately, the heat of the late afternoon had baked out any significant blue in the sky. The single wispy, whitish cloud in Marsha's vision gathered, and then was burned into oblivion. It was very much a symbol for her day, month, year, and life. Something which was almost there and then disappeared.

Marsha softly rubbed her palm along her thigh. The summer dress was smooth, but her memories of the night before were anything but. Her hand still felt warm from her father's touch.

The evening had been a pleasant surprise. As she walked into his hospital room, his head rolled and called her name. The voice was breathy, but he had distinctly said her name—not her mother's.

Putting her things on the chair, she had taken his hand. It was cool, but he had given her their secret double squeeze. She knew he had used the same secret squeeze with her mother, but she liked the memory of him crawling into her chair and blanket princess castle and explaining the secret squeeze. So even if he wasn't looking to see who it was, he knew and would squeeze back. She gave him the same double squeeze. His smile was as small and relaxed as hers.

The voice was low and more air than noise. "Princess…?"

"Yes, Daddy?"

His jaw thrust minutely forward toward the small cabinet of drawers and sink. "Over there in my pants pocket is some money. You take some and run down to the liquor store and get me a beer—I'm parched, and we're all out." His eyes and head rolled toward her. "Take a little extra and get a soda for you too…"

Kit turned around from the monitor. The look was one of question. Marsha shook her head as she told her father she would be right back with a cold beer. She jerked her head at Kit as she walked toward the door.

"Did you fetch him beer when you were a kid?"

Marsha's eyes drooped. "We all did. It was always a company town and a company store. Us kids fetched our father's beer, and nobody thought twice about it. It just ran the family deeper into debt to the company. It was cheaper to go down the mountain and buy anything, but it was more convenient to send the little pegs down and let them thumb their marker."

"Thumb their marker…?"

"If we didn't know how to write or sign our name, you inked up your thumb on the stamp pad and left your thumbprint where they told you to."

"Couldn't yet write…? That's some pretty young kids buying beer…"

"Many of them thumbprints were the size of grown men…" Her one eye challenged the nurse.

Kit backed off. "Okay… but that's not why you nodded for me to follow you…"

"How much would it hurt him to have a beer right now?"

"He's on a low dose of morphine with the machine—"

Marsha cut her off, "But would it hurt him?"

The word was as small and silent as the pursed lips and the slight shake of the head. "The man is on his deathbed."

"Where can I go buy a beer?"

Kit took a deep breath. "Last cooler in the cafeteria… Bud is on the top-shelf, and I think Coors is on the bottom shelf."

Marsha half turned. "Can I get you anything?"

Kits face opened in shock. Her mouth hung half-open—frozen.

Marsha realized what she had said, and the context. She laughed as he grabbed the nurse's arm. "Silly… I mean like a yogurt or some snack."

Kit relaxed and chuckled lightly as her head turned and she looked out the side of her eye. The two knew the look.

Marsha shrugged her face and rolled her eyes. "…unless you *wanted* that cold silver bullet?"

Kit pushed lightly at the other's arm. "Stop, and go be a bad girl. I'll finish here, and you two will have a couple of hours alone."

Marsha leaned in with a quick hug. "Thank you."

She had poured out half the beer in the public bathroom, but he didn't notice. He suckled on the straw like a calf to its mother. The transformation was good for him, and she had smiled as she remembered many evenings of the man and his one beer as he listened to the radio.

There was a small smile on his face. His eyes weren't focused. Marsha was sure he was listening to the radio again. She could almost feel the rag-braided rug coiled underneath her as she played with the blocks of wood with her brother.

A diesel truck passed her car. The car rocked with the wash of wind and Marsha returned to her driving.

She hated driving long distances. She particularly hated driving this stretch of the interstate. I-5—it didn't even have a nice name. It was built as utilitarian as its name. Someone named 'X' drew a line from San Diego through the deadest center of California, continued through the most populated section of Oregon, and finally reached the other side of Washington, saying they could build a highway along 'Y' location, for 'Z' amount of money. The idiots in Washington DC cheered, the fools in the three states said we can get it out of the taxpayers. And so the I-5 was built. And she was now on it.

The morning had started only one step off. The heel of her left shoe was torn off by a piece of metal at the gas station. Like most mothers who live their lives being prepared, there in her earthquake readiness box in her trunk was her spare set of shoes. The same set she had bought fourteen years before to go hiking with her son. The three-mile hike had convinced the young boy he didn't want to have anything to do with Cub Scouts. The week had led to a month, and then the JC Penney's wouldn't take them back. So they had rested in the bottom of the trunk, next to the space blanket, flares, snakebite kit, flashlight with dead batteries, and the box of half-eaten energy bars.

The other ladies in the school office had looked, shrugged, and said nothing. Marsha believed it would have been better if they had indulged in some camaraderie style ribbing.

It didn't happen. She wasn't part of the group. In fact, none of them had formed any kind of group. They took lunch at their desks or went in rotation. There was nothing to give them cause to bond. Nothing in the last eighteen years… Marsha stopped thinking about it.

Four kids sat on the long bench—waiting for their fates. One sat at the farthest end, his face speckled with the red dots of chicken pox. Why the nurse had installed him on the bench to wait for his mother was beyond Marsha. The other three clustered at the other end—waiting for the principal. Marsha knew the faces. They would continue to be regulars no matter what the principal said to them.

The one window was open two-inches as a nod to the early spring. God forbid we let any real fresh air into the old building. The oldest office staff pulled her heavy wool cardigan tighter about her neck and glared at the young one who was flapping her neckline. At fifty-two, the youngest of the office women might be joining the older ones a little early. *Lord knows she has been excessively bitchy as of late.*

"Marsha…?"

Marsha kept counting and turning the forms. *73, 74, 75…*

"Marsha, there is a Ulysses Doll on line one for you."

Marsha looked up. She frowned as she looked around. Ethel held up her phone. "A Ulysses Doll asked for you. He's on line one."

Marsha looked at the blinking button on her phone. She knew a Ulysses Trall…

She pushed the button and picked up her handset. "This is Marsha…"

"Marsha, this is Warden Ulysses Trall." He hesitated.

"Yes, Mr. Trall. Is there a problem?"

"There was a riot at breakfast. I'm afraid your son was just in the wrong place at the wrong time. How far away are you?"

Her shoulders slumped. She sat heavy in her chair. "It would take me at least four hours to get there…"

She could hear him talking to someone else. The sound had the echo of tile or steel walls. She could hear his unshaved beard scrape on the phone. "The doctor says to please hurry. I'll stay, so come to the administration entrance on the east side."

She didn't even remember hanging up. Her next memory was sitting next to a scared boy who didn't understand why she had come into the vice principal's office and just sat down crying. The man grabbed at his tie and jerked his thumb while telling the kid to get back to class and behave.

Vice Principal Hunsucker sat beside her and just let her cry. His arm was draped over her shoulders as she fell against his chest. He was the first man to understand Marsha without her even saying a word.

He had heard her out between the jagged hiccups and slowly drying tears. Within the hour, she was on the interstate.

The late afternoon sun was almost behind the high walls of the prison. She waited until the door buzzed. The muscular guard stood relaxed as she came through the door. His smile was a mix of recognition and sadness for the woman and the reason she was there. Many had come to know this quiet mother and had even tasted her cookies she would bring for Christmas. It made her sad anyone would have to work on the day no matter what the reason or job. She always had a kind word for the guards she had come to know. She explained it was not their fault her son was in their care.

"Good afternoon, Marsha. We're all very sorry you had to come for this reason." All the guards had learned years before she wanted none of the formality they all had to tolerate day after day. She only wanted first names and a bit of friendship—something lacking in prisons… or sometimes, in an office.

"Gerardo, how are you?" She knew she couldn't touch him.

"I'm fine. How was the drive?"

"Hot and longer than I ever want..." Her face lit up. "How is that boy of yours?"

The man's smile grew. "He is getting huge. He knows his alphabet now and can write his name, so he is all set for the fall when they start kindergarten."

She offered out her purse. He took it and handed it to the guard behind the acrylic shield wall.

"The warden is up in the hospital wing. He said to bring you right up so we don't have to go through the other stuff." He turned, and as they walked down the hall, he asked the important question. "Are you hiding any weapons on your person?"

Marsha smiled softly as she rolled her eyes. "Only the chainsaw I always have in my thigh holster."

He looked over at her. "You seem to be walking a little better than usual. How is your knee doing lately?"

"I've been getting a lot more walking in this last

month. My father is dying, and I park in the furthest parking lot and walk. The walking seems to lubricate the knee or something. Even the three sets of stairs aren't as grueling as they were the first week. Who knows, if he lives another year or two, I might take up running one of those marathons."

Against all regulations, he stopped and reached out his hand. His grip on her arm was as light as a feather. "I am so sorry to hear about your father. I can't imagine what you are going through right now. If I was losing my little peeper… or my father…" He collected himself and realized where his hand was. He squeezed lightly and let it fall. "I'm so sorry for your two losses."

She looked down and then back up. Her voice was halfway toward cracking. "Thank you, Gerry."

They walked the rest of the way in silence. They were buzzed into the room.

The man in a suit and tie stood. Marsha always wondered if he lost his hair from the stress of the job or just pulled it out. The man had a pencil line of a mustache half as thick as his narrow eyebrows.

"Marsha…"

"Ulysses." She nodded. "How is my son?" She knew everyone was aware they were on a first name basis, but she also knew better than to show more personal association when any of the staff was around.

The doctor stepped out of the bathroom area which had no door. "I'm sorry, Mrs. Arkadi, but your son probably won't see midnight. His kidneys are failing faster than his spleen."

The warden cleared his throat. "Marsha, this is Doctor Kaczynski."

She turned to face the man who had pronounced her son's death while the young man lay eight feet away. The insensitivity was beyond any she had ever experienced. She held her hands to her side. "I'm pleased to meet you… I believe you had a brother named Ted?"

The man started. "No… people confuse our names…"

She narrowed her eyelids and ground her head into a threatening cock. "Indiscriminately mailing death is no less inhumane than acerbically pronouncing death to a mother who is standing mere feet from her only son."

The man fumbled. "I didn't mean to—"

She cut him off with a chop of her hand through the air. "Your services are finished here, doctor. We will notify you when you can start cutting up the corpse."

The doctor looked for help from the warden. The warden remained motionless as the guard opened the door and waved the doctor to leave. The doctor's white smock flared as he turned and stalked out. The door closed a little more than quiet.

The warden closed one eyelid as he rolled his eyes. "If it weren't so darn hard to get any kind of doctor here…"

Marsha patted him on the arm as she passed around

behind him to her son. She wasn't sure if he was still alive. She sat and took his hand. The hand gripped back a double squeeze.

The eyes fluttered. The voice was soft but still her son. "I'm sorry, mom. I was being good."

"Hush, you were fine. Accidents are not of your control." She looked up to the warden. "What happened?"

"Two of the gangs started at each other during breakfast. The biker gang started—"

"To my son." Her face was a work of passive malevolence.

"A plastic shiv cut his spleen in half. Recently, they have taken to making them dirty…"

"What does that mean?"

The guard stepped over. He knew he had more contact with the woman than the warden. "They make the knife rough, and then wipe it down with their poop. The E. coli festers for a few weeks, and it can't be beaten with any known antibiotics. So even if the shiv doesn't do the job…"

The woman sighed angrily. "The shit finishes it."

The two men nodded.

The warden poked at the guard as he watched the woman. "We'll leave you alone with your son. The bathroom is there, and we'll send you up some dinner in about an hour."

Marsha sat back. She knew what she was there for. She had been practicing for the last month. *Maybe all my life…*

There wasn't much for them to talk about. Those days had ended when he turned thirteen and walked out the door. The person who came back home was not the one she had raised. The two girls had become sour or needy.

She examined the hand she loosely held. The long, slender fingers reminded her of the hand she had held so very long ago.

THE SERVICE ON the main floor of the church was always loud with the moaning and groaning, the screams of praise, and the talking in tongues. The minister had resorted to using a microphone with large loudspeakers. To sit in the large room was to hear nothing. The noise was a crash of cockamamie smaller crashes of each person going through their own experience of what they thought was communication or worship. The deafening noise reminded Marsha of the sound the chainsaw made just before the tree broke her knee.

She had escaped to the sanctuary of the quieter basement and Alexander.

The quiet, sullen boy had moved to Wasco a few years before with his family. His father rode the company bus up to the foothills to work in the gas field. The family had migrated from the Ukraine to the gas fields of Mexico and then driven to the border and asked for asylum. His father was an engineer and valuable. His mother had never wanted to leave the Ukraine and refused to learn English. Alexander had to take her everywhere to translate, something he would always resent. With people screaming nonsense in the service, his mother felt right at home—Alexander was not needed.

The boy of the Russian family became the nice boy of those Ukrainian immigrants at church. Marsha's father saw the sullenness as being a deep thinking Russian mind. Her mother only commented on how he kept his hair neat and short—unlike the wild ones she saw on the news or in town. It was never clear as to where she was viewing a television with its news. The radio was only ever turned to her father's bible station because they played nice music. Marsha ignored the inflamed preaching with how all the sinners were sure to burn in hell. She knew what fornication was, and her father drank and smoked, but the other stuff was not in the dictionary at school. She was certain that if she didn't know what the man was ranting about, her father certainly did not as well. He would simply nod and parrot whatever he had last heard the man on the radio say. After all, if the man wasn't important, he wouldn't be on the radio.

The two fathers were of the same liking. The louder the service, and the louder the congregation, then the closer to salvation they must be. Soon, the nice boy had a name in Marsha's house, and the pressure to invite him for Sunday dinner was on. There didn't seem to be any other nice boys at the church. Her father had spoken, and anything outside the church was not even up for discussion. Marsha was, at sixteen, rapidly approaching her maturity. Her mother was only seventeen when they had married.

Marsha was never assured it had been a marriage of love. The time between the wedding and her older brother's birth was never discussed. Marsha learned early about how things were when her mother's mouth became like steel, and her father stopped talking and sat down in his chair to turn on the radio. He had spoken.

Alex came to dinner.

It was never a romance. It was an escape from his mother and her father. Any time alone was viewed with a jaundiced eye… but any time they spent together had the blessing of both houses.

The time spent in the basement of the church was one of those moments. As the storm raged above, the two simply sat exhausted from the morning's intensity. Marsha marveled at some of the other girls at school talking about how long the hour of church service was. Marsha had never been to a church which wasn't nearly all-day.

When they had started kissing, Marsha couldn't remember. The kisses were dry and mechanical. It was more of the expected instead of the wanted. The kissing led him to assume he was free to fondle her sweater.

Her insistent taking of his hand and guiding it back to her side was only endured for a couple of minutes. The hard groping had occasionally become painful, and she begged to go to the toilet.

She quickly learned the toilet was no reprieve. If she sat in the stall too long, he was not beyond intruding into the sanctity of the women's room. He knew there would be no other women in the room, and it would only provide him with a smaller area in which to have his way with her.

She had really needed to pee. It took too long, and as she was wiping herself, he swung open the stall door with no locks.

Her dress was about her waist, and her white panties and tights were at her ankles. Her eyes were wild with fear or embarrassment—his were filled with lust.

She knew in her heart, even if she screamed, there was nobody who could hear or help her. The toilet was directly under the main cluster of the screaming mass above.

She tried to keep her legs together. His knee slid down hard between her thighs. His hand gripped her jaw tightly as his hard lips mashed on hers. He slapped her hard. The heel of his hand was more of a dull bludgeon on her jaw. It had hurt for weeks.

"Stop wiggling. I am the man. This is my right."

After she had cleaned herself up as best she could, he had taken her hand. He never let it go for the rest of the afternoon. He had all but dragged her upstairs as the sound of the service subsided into preparing for the community lunch in the gathering room.

He marched her up to her father and announced they were to be married. She was as shocked as everyone else. She had seen a shudder of fear in her mother. Her father had paused and then nodded. They sat in the center of the noise of the afternoon service. She never looked up. For the whole of the afternoon, she stared at the hand gripping hers. The symbolism was not lost on her. She would never escape.

THE HAND SHE now held had no grip left. It had long started to cool. She didn't want to lose yet another piece of her life. Her hand was frozen in time around the small hand of a twelve-year-old. They had gone up to the State Fair in Sacramento. There was a park with an undulating path that wound among nursery rhyme statuaries. He had loved them as a small boy, and he wanted to walk the path one last time. She had held his hand for old times' sake. They laughed and even had chocolate dipped ice cream cones. The day was perfect. It had been the last one of those days.

The small tapping on the high window drew Marsha's attention. A tiny sparrow had gotten through the wire mesh covering the bars and chicken wire enforced windows. It was building a nest against the window. *Life is so resilient but on the other side of the window.*

She let the hand slip from hers. She stood and gathered her sweater with the patches on the elbows. She patted her hand across the forehead and over the prison cut hair. She hadn't been allowed to touch him for over ten years.

She turned to the door. The prison could bury their prisoner—she had lost her son long ago.

09 Second Grip

MARSHA STARED AT the dark red pantsuit. It perfectly matched the expensive shoes, the band on the gold watch, as well as the ever-present red leather briefcase with the three gold embossed letters. There had never been any meat on the bones of her oldest. There had never been any meat to her life—no juice, no sauce, no spice or flavor. Everything had been to the sterile bone with her.

Even when Tiffany was a child, Marsha had shopped the women's petite section and then stayed up late taking in the extra fabric hanging from the shoulder blades. When other girls wanted cute print dresses, Tiffany had insisted on slacks or at least capris. Her blouses were to be solid color and opaque to not show even a hint of anything beneath.

Sometime in early high school, she had discovered singlet underwear. The lack of the usual telltale lines showing through her clothes had made her a convert. Marsha was certain she had never stopped wearing them.

The red jacket hung loosely down the middle of her back. The helmet of short dark hair was unmoving. Marsha leaned against the doorjamb watching the woman watch her grandfather.

Marsha knew the woman in red would never venture closer to the man. Somewhere in her, a part smiled knowing the man lying in bed was glad his granddaughter would never come closer. It was a standoff of emotions and generations. The young woman was afraid of catching something, and the old logger was just as afraid.

Marsha had gotten home from the prison at three in the morning. Her sleep had been that of the dead, but still, unrewarding. Her mood was not sympathetic.

"You can get closer and kiss him on the cheek." The woman flinched at the sound. "He isn't going to get up and chase you around the room like he did when you were five."

The lawyer wasn't going to give her the satisfaction of turning around. "They called me. They said they couldn't reach you."

Marsha pulled the phone out of her jacket and flipped it open. Dead.

"I turned it off. I was busy."

"Filing another nasty report on a child?"

Marsha was beyond fighting. Her child's caustic words didn't even give her a twinge. As she walked past the young lawyer, she mildly commented, "I see you have dandruff again."

She continued to the chair while the lawyer first bristled and then began pulling at her suit coat—checking for the telltale white dots. Marsha smiled at her father's limp face. She could see the tension near the one side of his mouth. He too was enjoying the granddaughter squirming.

Marsha carefully folded the cardigan and placed it next to her purse on the small table to the side of the bed. She thought about how the table hadn't been there before. *Kit*. Smiling at her father, she took his hand and leaned over to kiss him on the cheek. She paused at his head. "When you get to heaven, your grandson will be there to meet you. He left last night."

She gave the hand a double squeeze. The hand squeezed back.

He was awake.

She collapsed into the chair with a deep sigh. One more deep breath and she turned to look at her daughter. The woman was still trying to find the white flecks her mother had commented on but were not there.

"Tiffany Anne, stop it."

The woman straightened and glared. "Mother, you have no idea how hard it is. One little—"

Marsha sliced her off with her flat level hand in the air. "Stop."

"Mother—"

"Stop, I said. You don't get to run on about you. When I say stop, I mean it."

The woman pushed her weight back on her heels and squared her shoulders. "What?"

Marsha lowered her voice and softened it. "Now, what did they call you about?"

Tiffany started to hyperventilate as she pointed at the man in the bed. "He… they said he…"

"Stop." Marsha waited. "Calm yourself. Your grandfather has a name. He can be Grampa, PaPa, Grumpy, or Ted… but he has a name. I don't care if you want to separate yourself from this family… gosh knows, right now, I wish I had done so forty years ago. But, as long as my father is still alive, we are family. After that, you can go off and be a lone elephant roaming in the jungle. I don't care."

Marsha could tell her daughter was shifting into her courtroom persona. Whether she had actually been in a court was none of her concern. But if she ever was, or did, she was prepared.

"The hospital called me, saying my grandfather was in respiratory distress and needed my okay to let them help him. I gave them permission to treat him as needed."

Marsha froze.

The hospital had a POLST notice. He was not to receive any heroic measures such as cardiac shock or even CPR. He was to receive oxygen, pain medicine, and made to be comfortable. Anything else went against the Physician Orders for Life-Sustaining Treatment.

Out of the corner of her eye, Marsha noticed Kit in the hallway next to a cart. She was prepping a syringe.

Kit swept into the room with the syringe held high in her gloved hands. "Good evening, everyone. Sorry I'm late. This won't take but a moment." As she stuck the syringe into the IV port, she took in the lawyer and her perfectly appointed appearance.

"Taffy, dear, I think you might want to stand somewhere else. We think Teddy's little tum-tum is overly full of rotting festered bile and this is going to help him throw it up. Usually, it turns into some far-reaching projectile vomit full of hydrochloric and sulfuric acids that, when mixed with the amino acids, can and will bleach out that deep red in your jacket, or even on your shoes."

She turned toward the man and cheerfully asked, "Are you ready?" She plunged the syringe as Tiffany grabbed her briefcase and fled.

The man in the bed started to convulse. Kit gave it a three-count as Marsha started to rise. Kit waved her down as she leaned over to the man. "You can stop now. She's long gone."

The man continued to laugh until he started coughing. Kit raised him up to almost sitting up and adjusted the oxygen tube in his nose.

"Calling her Taffy was good... damn good." He head rolled toward his daughter. "But the lone elephant wandering the jungle almost had me lose it."

Marsha leaned back with her eyelids lowered.

"What is going on?"

Kit put up her hands. "It was before I came on. We had a young temp nurse. Evidently, old grumpy here didn't like her…"

"She was manhandling my privates."

Kit patted his chest. "She was giving you a sponge bath." She turned to Marsha. "She may or may not have touched his possible. She is only supposed to wash down as far as possible and up as far as possible. Washing possible is only legal in the state of Nevada and appears as a very different charge on your credit card statement."

He growled at her. She ignored him but held his hand. "She had laid him flat, and he started choking on the fluids in his esophagus. All she had to do was sit him back up, but she panicked. By the time they spoke to Tiffany, and she was on her way, I had come on the floor and bee-lined for the crowded room. Because, if anyone was shooting craps, I have a five buried in my shoe."

Marsha was laughing quietly and holding her side. She had forgotten how much this woman could be serious and still deliver some of the wackiest takes on what was happening.

"So the POLST wasn't broken?"

"Oh, honey, we done killed that POLST, plucked it, and roasted it last night. Where were you?"

Marsha wanted to laugh. It just wouldn't come. "I was holding my son's hand as he lay dying in prison."

Kit's mouth opened and then slowly closed. She looked at Ted and back at Marsha. "Oh, that is the worst." Her eyes were all questions.

Marsha gently shook her head. "It wasn't his fault. There was a riot in the cafeteria, and he got caught in the middle. There was nothing he could have done."

The clock ticked, and Kit looked up. Checking it against her watch, she withdrew the syringe. She held it up toward Marsha's questioning furrowed brow.

"Saline. It moves some things right along." She pulled the sheet and patted Ted's chest. "Look, I've got lunch in about forty. Are you up for a talk?"

Marsha nodded.

The cafeteria was busy. Marsha looked around at the other nine people. Only one was in nurses' scrubs. The man's top was puppies playing at being a doctor. Marsha hoped he was in the children's ward.

"If you are wondering, Cliff is in the newborn intensive care unit, but he also is the proud new daddy of seven cute new children."

Marsha's eyes were wide as she turned around. "Seven?"

Kit nodded. "And I have my eye on one of the white ones. Relax. They are Labrador Retrievers."

She sat as they both laughed. Kit waved her fingers at the other nurse. The man pointed to his chest at a white dog.

Kit smiled and gave him the thumbs up.

Kit cocked her head and made her one eye large.

"What? I wanted a kid…"

Marsha put out her hand in a stop. "It's fine… I… well, I really don't know much about dogs. But I would have pegged you more for a German Shepard or a big goofy fluff dog."

The blonde picked at her frosted tips of her hair. "I wanted something color-matched to my hair. Maybe next month I'll go for the big black spit monster—the big huggable bear looking ones."

"Not a wiener dog?"

"I'm not a wiener kind of girl." The two squealed with wide eyes and mouths.

Cliff walked by with his chest full of dogs. "You two are having too much fun, and the fun police are going to come down here and make sure you're not double punching your fun card."

Kit laughed and grabbed his hand. "Cliff, this is my friend Marsha. Marsha, this is the foster daddy to my baby."

"Nice to meet you."

Marsha leaned back and looked at the burly man who could have been mistaken for a logger. "So we were talking about preferences. Have you ever been a wiener kind of guy?"

"Oh, lord, honey—and we just met. Of course… ever since the sixth grade."

Kit leaned over as she held her side. "No, Cliff, she means dogs… wiener dogs."

The man turned with a horror-struck face. He held

his hands out about the length of a hot dog. "You're talking about bait? Little yappy bait dogs? Oh, heavens no. I go for dogs that are good for heat in bed or bears."

Kit chuckled as Marsha choked up. "Speaking of Justin…"

"Oh, gawd, girl… We shouldn't get me started. He is being such a butthead. I hid all of his razors, and he's still sneaking more home." He glanced at his watch. "Oh, looky there. Time to scoot. Nice meeting you, Marsha. Good to see Kittie is getting some therapy for that depression."

Kit swung her hand at his behind as he turned. "Go do something worthwhile. Make my child proud of you."

He danced through the tables and chairs as he raised his arm and index finger. "Saving the world one heartbeat at a time."

Marsha collapsed on the table. "What a character."

Kit deadpanned as she watched the door. "The most depressed man I ever want to know."

She looked back at Marsha and smiled. "Welcome to my friends."

"Newborns, huh?"

"He told me once a ten-pound baby girl was the most woman he ever wanted to handle. It looks so strange watching those huge hands handling a baby that fits in only one. But he is the best we have—possibly the best in the valley."

Marsha watched her until she had shifted gears

back to them. "What about my father?"

Kit took a large bite of her wrap and chewed. Finally, she sipped on her coffee and looked at Marsha.

"Fuck you. Not until you explain where you were last night."

Marsha was stunned. She had never been spoken to like that—other than by her husband. She blinked a few times. "Why?"

"Because you missed the most lucid time he has had all week. It was probably the last time too."

"He seemed pretty good this evening."

"No, tonight he is parroting. He isn't having a real thought. It's just a continuation of a running commentary of what someone else said or did. Last night, he was telling stories that had meaning and purpose. He talked about why he married your mom and how he always felt trapped with all the kids—but what he really wanted to do was go to sea. They were solid stories."

Marsha looked down at the tray in front of her. "Did he mention his grandson?"

"No. Why?"

"Because he passed away last night." There was only a small waver in her voice at the end.

Kit sat back and slumped. "Oh crap… I didn't think you were serious…" She squirmed in her seat and then leaned forward. "I am so sorry."

Marsha sat looking at her. She saw real caring in the woman's eyes… something she had not seen for many years.

"What about my father?" Her voice was quiet. The caring in the woman's eyes had taken her back to her wedding. Onna had come, and as they cut the sheet cake from Safeway, she had seen the same look in the eyes of her friend from drama class.

"This afternoon, hospice did an evaluation on him and recommended he be removed from glucose. Tonight he is still on a reduced drip of saline, but in the morning, they will remove his IV, and we will let nature take its course. I'm sorry this all comes at the same time…"

Marsha nodded as she thought. "Sometimes things happen for a reason. We don't see them for what they are at the time… it is only later we see them for the lesson or change we needed."

Kit glanced at her watch. "I hope this is one of those changes you need." She stood. "I've got to get back up there."

Marsha waved her off. "I've got some thinking I need to do. You go ahead. I'll stop in before I go."

She watched the fitted dark blue scrubs as she walked away, but it was the eyes she saw—except they belonged to a seventeen-year-old girl in a pink dress.

There were five tiny white baby carnations in her hair.

There was caring in her eyes, but the smile Marsha so desperately needed was gone.

They stood in front of the church, side-by-side, for

almost an hour. The entire time, all Marsha wanted to do was take her bridesmaid's hand. She wanted to hug her one more time. Kiss her one more time, and as she cut the cake of her marriage to a man of her father's choosing, she could tell in the deep blue eyes, the same was what her friend had wanted also.

10 Signing Off

THE MAN SMELT faintly of tobacco smoke, but he had a gentle smile. He turned through the next three pages and then pointed to the line. The process was, for the most part, silent except for the pen in Marsha's hand. The noise was scratchy like the ball had worn rough with use. She could feel the bite marks along the cylinder—it was far from new.

"And… finally here… and here."

She handed him back the pen. Why anyone in this day and age still wore a vest was beyond Marsha. The man gently clicked the pen closed as he stared at the final papers. Distractedly, he slid the pen into the top pocket of his vest.

He looked around the small house. It wasn't cluttered, but it wasn't empty either. "You're sure about all this…? I mean, the Salvation Army thanks you for your generosity and all… We just don't want to strip away your life…"

She held up her palm and let her eyelids nod. "I'm sure. The men were here yesterday to take the few things over to my daughter's new apartment. If your men find we missed anything with an orange sticker on it, just take it anyway. Lord knows, she won't miss what she never got.

His chest sagged as he turned back. "I just think it is the saddest thing when a person loses their home. I see it a bunch more than I want to these days."

"Mr. Greenwald, I'm not losing my home—I'm getting my own home. This here is just a house. It's a house full of memories. A few of them are good, but most…"

"But it goes to auction next week…"

"Yes, yes it does. I asked for it to be put up for auction."

"But if you listed it—"

"Some smart person would snap it up for more than I need." She reached out and covered his hand. She could see he was having a hard time with the idea, and it disturbed him. "I figured, at an auction, there might be a few people bidding who really need this house. I surely hope they beat out the bloodsuckers who would just tear this old home down and build something bigger. Worse yet would be a developer who tore it down to build a stupid apartment building to ruin the neighborhood. This is a nice simple neighborhood, and this home needs a happy family with a couple of happy kids in it."

The man stood as his head bobbed listening to her words and weighing their value in his outlook on life.

"Well, it is certainly your house to do with." He looked her clear in the eyes. "I'll pray on it until the sale. I have a feeling you have a good heart, and I hope the guy up above is listening. For this neighborhood, this house, and some nice young family just starting out, I hope you're right."

Marsha stood and grabbed his hands. "Everything has a purpose, Mr. Greenwald, and in my heart, I feel the purpose of this house is to go to a young loving family."

His head bobbed quietly as his lips rolled in at this thought. He looked up, but she could see his eyes had taken on a slight wetness. "So what will you do now?"

Marsha chuckled softly as she walked them out the front door. She pointed at the street. "You see that camp bus… that is where I am. I have three months rent paid on it. With luck, it will be enough time to go find out what's next."

"Where are you going to go?"

She pointed down the street. "You see the stop sign two blocks down?"

"Yeah…?"

"At the stop sign, I have three choices. I can turn left, right, or just keep going straight. Tomorrow morning, I'll go find out which of those sounds good."

The man laughed. "Can I give you a hug?"

She opened her arms and smiled. The extra wetness in the eyes seemed to be going around.

He just hung in that hug. "Until five seconds ago, I

thought I knew what I was about. I thought I even knowed what I was doing waiting for my retirement. All my life has been about planning." He gently took her shoulders in his hands and pushed her back a foot. "And then, here you are. You done give it all away so someone lesser could have a chance at happy. You aren't even sticking around to see it happen—you're just trusting it, too. In the morning, your way will be shown you, and you just trust in that, too…"

Marsha started to speak. She cleared her throat. "All my life, I've heard preachers talk about a leap of faith. But I also heard them beg for more money in the offering plate and making plans. I have done what I was told to do and how it would all work out. Well, Mr. Greenwald, it didn't. So now I'm going to hold my nose and just step off the cliff and see where my next step lands. Tomorrow is everything I haven't tried yet, so it can't be any worse than all my past, can it?"

He hesitated and then gently placed his palm on her upper chest. "You have a heart so big, this body can't contain it, and it gots to get out. I think tomorrow is the beginning of a new life, and if you keep up this way, it will be a good one."

She hugged him again and then he was gone. She closed the house up and put the key in the lock box. She had lied to the man. The stop-sign was ten minutes away.

The bus turned left.

"MAR MAR, MY mama says that you come now so we can eat." The young boy was out of breath more from internal agitation than from physical exertion.

Marsha laughed as she dried her hands. "Peter, you need to stand still, honey bunch. You're getting all worked up and then you will need a spray from your inhaler." She stepped down and closed the door. "Besides… you know what?" She bent slightly and took his hands.

"Wh… wha… what?" His almond shaped eyes were almost round in excitement.

"I'm hungry, and I have a handsome young man taking me to dinner." She smiled at his rounded mouth.

"W… wh… we have to go before mama feeds your steak to a bear."

"Now, which mama is going to feed that there bear?"

"Mama."

"Which one, Peter? You have two of them."

"Mama Leslie."

Marsha laughed. "Well, let's go see if she found a bear and I lost out on a steak."

Hand in hand, they walked around the thick wall of the giant fennel separating the two campsites.

Marsha leaned down a bit to be at the young boy's height. The Down's syndrome was only part of his makeup. His genetics had also gifted him with legs only half the length of his torso. He had the legs of a five-year-old, but the torso of his fourteen years. He quite possibly would never grow past his height of four-and-a-half-feet.

"So what did you do exciting today?"

Later, the three folding camp chairs lined along the edge of the cliff. The three women sat watching the end of the day as the sun slipped silently into the ocean off the Big Sur.

Marsha found the small campground on the map the week before. The ranger at Hearst Castle told her he had spent his honeymoon there. On a Friday afternoon, the sites were usually all gone by early afternoon. She pulled into her site on Tuesday afternoon. The licorice scent of the wild fennel was heady. That night, she had dreamed of penny candy, the smell of fresh cut sawdust on her father, and watching for the first chickadee in the winter snow.

She had gotten up in the middle of the second night to pee. She considered the strange smiling person in the mirror. The hair was a wild storm cloud of gray and black, but the smile was peaceful and happy. She slept until almost noon.

The following morning she met Leslie, Carol, and Peter as they pulled their RV into the next campsite. The two women had met in college and became roommates, then lovers, and finally, partners for life. Peter was a foster child because lesbians couldn't marry and single people couldn't adopt children. Carol joked the first night as they explained their situation. "We can run or own a business, we can buy buildings and homes, we can even drive cars, but we aren't stable enough to be an adoptive parent. For that, we have to have a piece of paper that says marriage on it."

Peter came into their lives at the age of three months. The birth mother told the hospital to take the baby and tell her husband it died in birth. A friend of theirs, who ran the newborn crisis center, mentioned the baby one night at dinner. The thought of a mother rejecting her child because of birth defects reminded Carol of her Hawaiian heritage, where the old practice was to either carry the newborn into the surf or throw them into a volcano. The thought of it happening in the twentieth-century was cause for long sleepless nights and conversations about who the two women really were. They had been partners for only twelve years, and both had very busy lives.

Leslie started the process for them to become foster parents. Carol started streamlining her many commitments. The result, much to their surprise and joy, was a lot more time for them and the baby they always thought of as their son.

"We missed you on the hike today." Carol's smiling face turned toward Marsha.

"I would have loved to, but I was out of food. I've learned my lesson now. When I finally found a market up in Monterey, I stocked up." She laughed lightly. "I was using their bathroom and realized there was only a tiny bit of paper left. If I had pooped, I would have done the dirty walk. Sitting there is when I remembered I was also down to my last roll in the RV."

The other two women laughed. "Been there."

Leslie leaned forward to look past Carol. "We went to Moab for two weeks when Peter was ten. He didn't remember about the stash under the sink. So he wiped himself with the tube."

As Marsha started laughing, Carol grabbed her forearm and added, "It gets worse. He knew better than to throw anything into the toilet that wasn't the special toilet paper... so he stood the roll up on the counter. Leslie found it about an hour later when she needed to go... and was going to teach him about putting up a new roll."

Leslie fell back snickering. "When I got to the part about where the extra rolls were... I opened the cabinet."

Marsha's mouth flew open, and she leaned forward and laughed. "It was empty."

Carol chortled. "Only the plastic wrapper. Which doesn't feel great when you need to pee." She turned to her partner. "Or so I've been told."

She turned back to Marsha. "In the morning, we'll show you the list we've built."

The misty golden ball of the evening sun touched the water and puddled gold across the ocean. The three sipped on their mugs of spiked hot chocolate. Watching a sunset with quiet self-reflection and relaxation was an important lesson the two women had taught Marsha.

They made a point of it whenever Peter had time away from his school, they were off exploring in an RV. Peter had driven them to explore thirty-two other states—twenty-eight more than his mothers had ever been to. They had t-shirts with a large capital 'T' and a small three: tee cubed. They called themselves the Third Traveling Tribe. Each person made up one-third of the tribe. To Marsha, after knowing them a week, she knew it meant they were all equal in every way.

In the calm of the evening dark, they still sat. The canvas and wood creaked as Marsha shifted. "You've traveled all over the country, but you always come here in the summer…"

Carol sipped the last of her cocoa. "It's always Peter's choice. Since he was six, we have gone where he wants to. We put up a map of the country in the office, and he throws a dart. If it is not near an orange sticker where we've gone before, we go."

"But you always come here."

"We found this on the map when he was nine. The dart landed out there in the water somewhere. We had a Volvo station wagon and a large tent then. I called the ranger station at Jade Cove, I think. The ranger was very nice and told me about the KOA camp and such. I told him we had a boy with special needs who loved nature and hiking. The man was quiet for a moment and then said his nephew had cerebral palsy, and when he was still able to walk with the braces and canes, he loved this place. The quiet is calming, and it all happens at their speed. We went to Disneyland one time. Peter loved it but was exhausted after two hours. We got a chair and pushed him around for another hour. He finally started crying—he wanted to go to a quiet beach."

"A quiet beach in southern California… I mean where do you find such a thing?"

"One of the older saleswomen told us about where her husband used to surf. It's a place called Crystal Cove. It was the perfect place. But when we found this campsite, Peter doesn't even throw the dart for summer anymore—he just sticks the dart in the old hole. We put a gold star next to the hole."

"So every summer, it's two weeks back here." Marsha smiled. She liked the idea. This past week had been good for her. She could feel the waist on her pants had grown loose. "So what happens when he's older?"

The two women looked at each other in the dimming light. Marsha wasn't sure who had reached for the other's hand first.

"Peter's condition is very complicated. You see his Down's syndrome and stunted legs, but the rest of his condition is inside. Due to various problems, his body is slowly tearing itself apart and killing him. Each and every day we still have him is a blessing. The doctors never expected him to be this old. This last year things have degraded to a point where we may not have him next summer. He doesn't understand why, but he's happy we are spending an extra week this year."

"I think I can understand. This spring, I held my son's hand as he died and then, four days later, my father. It's not something I will ever take lightly."

Carol's voice was low and broken. "Can we ask?"

Marsha thought about how personal it was and then about Peter. "My son was in prison. He got caught in a riot. They call the knife the prisoner's make from all sorts of things—a shiv. The plastic one he was stabbed with was plastic and broke off inside him. It had split his spleen, but also, they evidently rub the knives down with poop so the E. coli will kill the guy they stab."

She sighed. "My father was a logger all of his life. I'm sure the beer didn't help either, but what he died of was a few kinds of cancer that comes with the forest. In the logging world, we just call it Logger's Lung. There is no way to cure it because it's not just one thing. The lungs are failing while the heart is failing and the body is just worn out."

Leslie and Carol chorused, "Sorry."

In the dark, none could see the other weep.

11 A Fresh Grip

THE WOMAN WHO walked into the school office at the end of the summer was not the same one who had left three months before. Marsha was glad she had given away almost all of her wardrobe because none of it would have fit her new body or attitude now. Each of the women had to look twice at the redhead in the flowery summer dress.

Only the voice was somewhat the same—except the reticence was now gone. Even her walk had changed with the many miles of hiking trails and parks. Her stride was assured and confident. But for the women in the office, the most unnerving change was the smile on her face. She glowed with health and life.

The principal wandered out of his office as he read through a file. His steps were small, but he brushed against the woman walking toward a desk. Out of the corner of his eye, he took in the light dress and the red hair. He mumbled an apology as he kept walking. He made it to the swinging gate at the large counter. He looked up and out the office door at the empty hall.

"Marsha?" He turned around as the woman pulled her chair out.

"Yes?"

The man blinked a few times. His hand dropped to his side with the papers. The mother waiting with her daughter stopped, standing with her body hovering only a few inches above the bench. She sensed her turn had been usurped. She sat back down.

Marsha smiled as she slipped her small clutch into the bottom drawer. "You needed something, Phil?"

He and two of the women started at the use of his first name. "Um, could we talk in a few minutes?"

"Of course. I'm here all day." The smile on one side drew in tight. It wasn't quite a smirk, but more of an acknowledgment of the humor.

He smiled and bounced the edge of the file against his left palm. Marsha had seen the same in some of the older kids. It was a date. Not like a real date, but a small win.

She looked over the files on her desk. He turned to face the woman and child but cranked his head back to look at Marsha again. Marsha could sense the look. She smiled at the slight blush.

The principal gently closed the door of his office. "Welcome back. It looks like the time off did some good."

Marsha smiled and only blushed slightly. "It's okay, Phil. You can say it. I lost forty-three pounds, I can now hike five miles and enjoy it, my hair is red, and I love it, and the other women in the office are going to hate me either way. They always did, and now I don't even care about what they think."

The man had paused while sitting. He now plopped with both eyebrows tented. "Excuse me, but when did we let the wildcat in here?" He chuckled, but she could tell it was more from amazement and admiration than mockery.

"You have no idea, Phil. This summer I did things I only wanted to do. Most of them I didn't even know about until I did them or a few days before. I might even take up surfing."

"Surfing?"

She shook her head. "I sat on the cold sand watching surfers wax their boards in the gray predawn light. I watched them cluster offshore in camaraderie like a club. There were girls out there too, but it was all about them surfing. They cared about each other. When they came in on the beach, they watched each of the others. A young Filipino who had come to America last summer sat with me on the beach for a couple of hours. He explained the waves and what everyone was doing. Some of the other surfers would join us for a while and then go back out. I asked Juan why he was just sitting with me and he said because someone had sat with him once, and he had become a surfer."

"But he was just a kid…"

"No, he was a software designer and has two grandchildren."

The principal laughed. "What else did you do?"

"A lot of things I had never even thought of. I kissed a dolphin and a walrus in San Diego. I picked lettuce for an hour in the Imperial Valley and oranges in Riverside. I took a sailing lesson in San Diego and fed seagulls from my fingers in a quiet cove in southern California. I put my hands on the oldest tree in the world. I watched the sun come up across Death Valley. I panned for gold in the Gold Rush Country and rode in a jet boat on Lake Tahoe."

The man smiled. "Did you gamble at the state line?"

"I sure did. I ordered a Reuben sandwich at Harrah's Club. I think I could become an addict real easy. But in San Diego, a couple talked me into going for sushi with them. I think it beats the Reuben, but only by a smidge."

"So what now…?"

"Now it's back to work. I thought a lot about this all summer. I do like it here, but I'd rather work with the kids more, instead of just being one of the office ladies. I hated those old sourpusses when I was in school, and I'm sure they hate us now."

"What would you like to do?"

"Maybe some kind of an advisor. The kids hate us because we don't talk with them. You only see them when they have been bad. They will never know you only want them to succeed and be happy in their lives… and I don't want to be a party to that either. I want to be part of us talking with the kids, and them talking with us."

He pursed his lips and pulled on them with his finger and thumb. "Counselors have a lot of education, but maybe if we can create something more akin to a peer advisor…"

"I just don't want to shuffle files anymore. I want to get up and move… I want to do… I want to connect."

The man snorted with a smile. "You started moving, and now you're addicted and can't stop."

"I'm sixty-two. I was stopped all of my life. I need a new life, and if I can't find it here…"

He put up his hands. "I hear you. Let's work on this. But for right now I need you here in the office." His open hand floated up and down. "I need all of you. The fire in your hair, the fire in your walk, and especially the fire in your belly—I need… I mean, the school, the kids need all of what you have transformed yourself into."

As he opened the door, his voice lowered, "And, would you talk to my wife. Maybe you can get her moving…"

Marsha poked him in the tummy. "I think we will start with the two of us walking the track at lunchtime. Maybe if you show you're changing, she can join in."

He laughed. "We're going to have to change your name to Norma Rae."

She pushed her lips out flat and nodded. "Maybe

so… just maybe so."

She was sure the other office women hadn't moved or even breathed since they had entered his office and shut the door.

This office needs a lot more than Norma Rae ever did.

12 When Did You Know?

MARSHA SAT IN the parking lot of the hospital—thinking. She had been distracted all afternoon. A young girl was caught fighting, and from her dress, haircut, and bravado, Marsha had made a judgment about her. She didn't like making the judgment or the fact she would even make such a judgment.

The young girl was combative and evasive in the principal's office. The principal couldn't get a word out of her about what had started the fight or why. Even faced with the threat of suspension or expulsion, the girl was shut down.

The principal stepped out of his office and asked Marsha if she would call the girl's mother. Marsha had corrected the man. The mother was serving three to five years in Vacaville prison for aggravated assault. The biological father had always been absent or too many new daddies had been absent after short stays.

Marsha called the grandmother work. It had taken several minutes waiting for the woman to come to the business phone. Marsha explained the situation. She could sense the exhaustion and frustration in the woman's voice. The best the woman could do was talk to the girl when she got home from work—at eight that night or pick her up at the police station when she could get some money.

Marsha quietly offered to talk to the girl. The principal had waved her off distractedly, dismissing the offer as not part of her job. She leaned in and got his eye and attention. She didn't know where the courage or strength to do so had come from. Her voice was a low, quiet growl. "It may not be my job, but it damn sure is my responsibility."

She could see the man was on shaky new ground. He was no longer certain about what kind of woman worked in his front office, but he was certain that he wasn't going to let any chance get away. Marsha didn't need to remind him about their idea of her reaching out—their lunch-time walk on the track was now up to five staff and two students.

Marsha slipped into the principal's office carrying two sodas. She held one out as the middle finger of each hand snapped the pop-top on each can. She had always thought of it as one of her mom-style super powers.

The washed out green eyes of the young woman looked up. The pain around the temples was obvious to Marsha. She had seen the look many times around her own dead leaf brown eyes. The first time was looking in the mirror as she tried on the powder blue dress she had planned to wear to the prom when she was a little older than this girl.

The words slid out soft as the wings of a spring moth. "Oh, my God…" She softly sat down on the plastic chair next to the girl, pressing the cold wet can into her trembling hands.

Marsha took a deep breath. "Just drink. I don't want you to say a word you don't want to, but you can just listen to me first because I sat in that same chair a very long time ago."

The girl glanced up and flicked her head so the long hanging rope of a ragged bang flipped back up onto her head. As she looked back down at the can, the hair slid off and hung again—as was the nature of the haircut—part shaved head, part military short, and a small area hanging over one eye and into the face. Marsha inwardly referred to all the similar cuts as the 'I hate myself' haircut. Too many kids these days wore similar haircuts, clothes, and walked with a beaten or about to be beaten slump. The look was usually accompanied by an abusive, defiant, and foul mouth.

Marsha took a sip of the cloy-sweet drink. She had never taken to soda, but she didn't know if coffee would have been proper to offer.

"When I was your age, I had a friend. We had cleaned motel rooms during the summer. We found things people had left or forgotten. There were the odd pieces of clothes, the bra, panties, men's undershorts or undershirt. More often than you would think there were condoms—still in the packets or used. There were businessmen who forgot their paperwork or someone who forgot letters—some read, some old and worn but never opened. There were magazines. A woman may have bought a Cosmopolitan to distract herself with, or a man may have left his car or hunting magazine. Occasionally, there were some naughty magazines like a Playboy."

The girl glanced up. Looking through the narrow veil of hair, she gave a soft snort and then looked back down.

"We liked the Cosmos because there were dresses we would never wear. The photos were taken in places we could only dream of going, but knew we never would." She took in a breath and gave a soft sigh. "The dirty magazines we kept and hid to look at later. There were pictures of what we were hiding under our shirts. Even in the heat of the summer, the closest to naked we saw each other was short sleeve shirts and shorts down to here." She rubbed her hand along her thigh. "When we were alone, we taught each other about how to kiss. Or at least… that's what we told ourselves."

The girl wasn't laughing. She wasn't moving. Marsha could sense she was listening.

"When school started back up, we both took Drama class. We liked working as stage crew. In the dark of the backstage, during a play, we were hidden."

The girl murmured, "What happened?"

Marsha slouched in the chair. She let her

exhaustion take over. "Nothing. Nothing happened." She looked over at the girl. "We didn't know any more than what we were doing. Marches were something the band or the military did. Protest was what you cried when you thought your parents were unfair by sending you to bed without supper because you broke something. We didn't even have words for girls kissing girls or men with men. That all came after… after we had gone to war. It was after women burned their bras, stopped shaving their legs and under their arms because we no longer wanted to fit into the image of our mothers or what our fathers wanted us to be."

The girl sat up and set the untouched can of soda on the desk. The wet ring swelled into a puddle. Marsha fought the urge to find a towel.

The ink-marked hand smoothed the hank of hair back onto her head. "So what did you do?"

Marsha gently closed her eyelids as her eyes rolled. She blew a long slow breath out of her pursed lips. The weight of her life was heavy and present.

"I did what my father wanted. He liked a boy at our church. He urged me along until we were dating. The summer after we graduated, while women in Los Angeles were burning their bras on Hollywood Boulevard, and students were marching down Telegraph Avenue in Berkeley, I became Mrs. Alexander Arkadi." She sighed. "The bruises, drinking, and not coming home took up the next twelve years and three children."

"He beat you…" The girl looked back down.

Marsha was stunned by it being more of a tired statement than a question. This young girl had barely started her life and was already old and weary.

As Marsha nodded her head silently, she placed her can next to the other. Their rings merged into a larger puddle.

"And… you stayed…"

Marsha fell back tiredly. "It was my wifely duty. I had babies… they needed their mother."

"Even if it meant getting beat on…?"

"At the time, I didn't see or even know there was an alternative. It was what was expected of me. I was the good daughter and made my father and mother happy. Then I did what made my husband happy—"

She cut her off. "But you didn't want to be married. Not to a dude…"

Marsha thought a moment. "What color is the sky?"

"What does that have to do anything?"

Marsha looked her in the eyes. "What color?"

"Blue."

"How do you know it's blue?"

"Because …" The girl stopped. "Because that is what I was taught."

Marsha sadly rocked her head and upper body. "Because… it is what we were taught."

They sat there quietly—each with their own thoughts or new ones forming. The bell rang in the hall.

The sound of hundreds of feet and bodies thundered dully through the floor and walls. Marsha could sense the principal looking through the window from the outer office. She didn't turn her head.

"So, why are you telling me this?"

As Marsha sat thinking, the second bell rang. There was the sound of slapping feet running late to class. Her eyes ticked from wall to the ceiling, to the desk, and the floor. There was no clear answer.

"I don't know…" She began. Still searching, she continued. "Maybe… because it's a shitty world out there. I know I'm not supposed to say such things… but damn it all, maybe that's the problem. We, I, society… we've been doing what is right or expected of us—what we've been taught. But when do we get to do what is right for us—personally?

"There was an old story I heard when I was young. It was about a small bird who hadn't flown south for the winter. The bird was cold and lonely and then heard another bird singing. It was a happy song. Well, maybe not happy, more like sad but cheerful. He finally found the other bird. The bird had wallowed down into a large steaming pile of fresh steaming cow manure. The first bird asked the second bird why, when he was covered in shit, was he singing a cheerful song. The second bird replied because it is warm. The first bird thought about it, and then climbed in and wallowed until he was also covered. Soon they were both singing."

The girl snickered. "So it's okay to be covered

with shit…?"

Marsha nodded. "As long as you're warm." She reached over the few inches and took the girls hand. "I just want you to be warm—even if it's only for a little while. Eventually, the shit gets cold, but there is always a new fresh pile of shit somewhere."

The girl snorted softly as she shook her head. "That's a crappy way to look at life… but at least it's warm."

They sat there staring at the wall behind the large desk, neither speaking, just taking in the warmth.

Finally, the girl asked into the air in front of them—never turning her head, not confronting. "So… when did you finally figure out you were gay?"

Marsha almost jumped. She wasn't sure if it was the girl's voice or the voice in her mind—they were both asking the same question.

"I never did." She swallowed, but her voice was still wet and husky. "I think I'm still trying to figure it all out."

"So you just came out to a fucked up fourteen-year-old dyke…"

Marsha twitched at the swearing, and at the reality of what the girl was saying. "No… I think I just had a talk with another person who could also use a friend." She cleared her throat and turned to face the girl. Her lips curled up into a small smile, "… and yeah, maybe that too."

The large clock did the double-step click-clunk

above their head as the girl gently leaned over and rested her head on Marsha's shoulder. Marsha recognized the soft jerks which came with the silent crying of a young girl.

She had time.

She had all the time it would take.

13 Christmas in November

THE LARGE PACKAGE shimmered in wet-looking deep purple wrapping. The bow was a wide wire-reinforced ribbon of gold lace and satin. The small envelope was gold with a tiny embossed Christmas tree. The green tree and ornaments were hand colored to look cheery. The whole was happy and out of place in the oncology ward.

The man walked past a woman slumped in a wheelchair as he carried the package to the nurse's station. He stood quietly not knowing what to do. The nurse did not fit the description he had been given along with a name. Neither fit. The name tag said Pam.

She glanced and then did a double take. "May I help you?"

The young man in the courier's uniform stalled, and then read the card. "I'm looking for a nurse named Kit?"

"She doesn't come on for another twenty minutes. You can leave it right there, and I can sign."

"It's personal."

The older woman turned and jammed her fist down into her soft hip. She looked over her glasses at the man. The man squirmed under her glare. "Look, honey bunch, you are making a delivery in a community hospital. I'm old enough to be your grandmother. I have seen more weird shit than you'll even think of in the next fifty years unless you run off to San Francisco or Hollyweird. So you can either come back or leave it there… but don't tell me that it's personal. There ain't nothing personal on this floor. We watch people wet themselves, poop themselves, and drool into toilets on their way to dying. Personal is something that got checked at the door a long time ago."

"I'll just leave this right here." He placed the package as if it contained a bomb set to go off if jarred. He stepped back, turned, and fled from the crazy nurse on the strange dying ward. He almost ran into the bundled woman in the wheelchair on his way to the elevator.

Pam pushed her glasses up her nose and watched the way the funny young man walked fast. "Good choice, punkin'."

She went back to staring at the computer screen. The package was forgotten.

"Pretty package."

Pam didn't even glance up. She knew the voice. "It was left for Kit, Clemie. If you're on, would you be a dear and check the alarm in fourteen?"

"There's no alarm…"

The older nurse held up her left hand with four fingers. She counted down by curling each one at a time. Three-two-… "That alarm."

The young black nurse shook her head as she charged off down the hall. She passed the older nurse with the spiky frosted shag-cut hair.

"Mr. Ramirez pull his catheter again?" Kit laughed and didn't even slow down. She approached the red haired woman slumped in her wheelchair dead or asleep. Kit paused and felt the wrist. The pulse was there. "You'll live." She continued toward the station to check in.

"Evening, sunshine."

"Good morning, Pam. When did we inherit the redheaded hall creeper?"

"I noticed her about an hour ago. She's a slow mover so my guess is she crept over from the psych ward."

"Pretty package, but I think it's a little early for Christmas, isn't it?" Kit bent over and looked into the computer screen seeing which rooms were what.

"You're on the east side. You have six because I know Clemie can't handle more than five. But she had Chuckles."

"Yeah, I heard the alarm as I walked past. Anything I need to get on first?"

"Your package. Some young courier delivered it about half an hour ago. I done sniffed it… there's nothing to eat in there."

Kit frowned and moved to the package. She removed the card and opened the envelope. The purple card matched the wrapping. It all was so mysterious and yet elegant. Kit smirked. *This belongs in a Hollywood movie instead of a cowtown hospital oncology ward.*

She opened the card. *Kit, Your seamstress says these will fit. Thank you.*

She flipped the card over—nothing. She read it again and then put it down.

Thinking, she slid the ribbon off the box and slipped off the wrapping. The other nurse stood, now drawn in.

Kit removed the lid from the box and drew back the tissue paper. The scrub tops were her dark blue. There was another gold card.

She opened the card. *But you need color in your life also.*

She rolled the dark blue top forward to reveal a deep purple top. The purple revealed a deep carmine red top. Embroidered on the right chest was a green Christmas tree with ornaments. Just in case, she rolled the red top down, and sure enough, there was a green top. A stack of gift packages was embroidered on the chest. The packages were wrapped in blue, purple, and red with gold ribbons. A teddy bear leaned against the stack.

Kit wiped at her eyes. She didn't know what to do. The stitchery was getting blurry as if underwater.

The redhead in the wheelchair crept the last few feet and stood up as she placed the blanket on the chair. She stood smiling.

Kit wiped her eyes. There was something familiar about the woman standing there. Finally, she realized who it was. She stepped around the end of the counter and fell into the woman's arms crying.

Pam pulled a few tissues from the box before she snapped it down on the counter.

Smiling, Marsha grabbed a few and then grabbed a few more.

As she blotted at her eyes, Kit pushed back to arm's length.

"Goodness gracious. I would have walked right past you on the street."

"You did. I was sitting at the seamstress when you came in, picked up a set of scrubs and left. You even nodded to me for cutting in." She laughed, "You were so focused. I almost blew it by saying something."

Kit pulled the box of scrubs over. "But this is too much. You can't do this."

"Yes, I can. You did so much for my father and for me. But you really do need more color in your life."

Kit reached over to the long red hair. "Hmm, speaking of color… this looks really good on you."

"I'm still getting used to it. Sometimes I walk past a mirror, and it startles me. I was living in an RV in San Diego when I did it. I scared the crap out of myself more than a few times. RV's are a small area, and if you think you have an intruder—your heart can only take so much.”

Kit started looking at the dress. There was nothing dull or frumpy about it. “Look at this… what happened to the cardigan you wore…?”

“It went to its own hell. I stuck it in the bottom drawer of my dresser, and then I donated everything in the house to the Salvation Army. The following week they auctioned off my house. I’ve been by. A young couple got it. He works in the oil field, but he’s also with the Army Reserve. They have two little girls named Misha and Tawanda. They brought so much happiness to that house.”

“If you lost the house, where are you living?”

“I didn’t lose the house, I just let it go. For now, I’m living in a small apartment. But then, I have so much to tell you about. I’d really like to take you out to dinner some evening. Would you be up for that?”

Kit started to say something, and she stopped. She studied the woman’s face. This was a completely new woman standing in front of her.

“Does that mean you’re asking me out… like on a date?”

Marsha was slow to smile. “Yes, I guess it does.”

Books by the Authors

Shye Ryder

Making Mandi
What About Marsha?

Baer Charlton

Southside Hooker Series
1 Death on a Dime
2 Night Vision
3 Unbidden Garden
4 Boomtown
5 One Day Under the Grass

Literary Fiction
The Very Littlest Dragon
Stoneheart (2015 Pulitzer Nominee)
Angel Flights
What About Marsha